"As soon as you get it through your head that I'm only going to help you, you'll talk," Audubon said.

"I'll never trust you, because you'll never admit your motive," Elena said.

"You want a motive? Here." He took her by the shoulders, swung her to face him, wrapped one arm around her shoulders and another around her waist. With a suddenness that took her breath away, she was on her tiptoes, her body conforming to his from chest to thigh. She cursed the years of training that magnified every nuance of his body to her senses.

"When we danced the other night, I wanted you in a pure male-wanting-female way," he whispered, his voice angry and challenging. "And you wanted me. Don't tell me you didn't."

"It's not enough."

"I don't have many personal pleasures in life, believe it or not. I want to feel the way you make me feel, Elena."

His mouth took control and twisted his lips on hers. There were dozens of emotions and sensations in the contact—the warm push and pull of his mouth, the shivers of pleasure. Fear shattered as intimacy brought them so close it seemed impossible to think of distrusting him again. But it was easy to be deceived. . . .

"You want to play games?" she asked, reaching beneath his shirt to caress his chest. "I have power, too," she warned. "A different kind." This time he was the one who drew a sharp breath. "Part of your life belongs to me now," Elena whispered, letting her heat and energy pour out. "Now I know you in a way that no other woman will ever know you. . . .'

## WHAT ARE *LOVESWEPT* ROMANCES?

They are stories of true romance and touching emotion. We believe those two very important ingredients are constants in our highly sensual and very believable stories in the *LOVESWEPT* line. Our goal is to give you, the reader, stories of consistently high quality that may sometimes make you laugh, sometimes make you cry, but are always fresh and creative and contain many delightful surprises within their pages.

Most romance fans read an enormous number of books. Those they truly love, they keep. Others may be traded with friends and soon forgotten. We hope that each *LOVESWEPT* romance will be a treasure—a "keeper." We will always try to publish

*LOVE STORIES YOU'LL NEVER FORGET*
*BY AUTHORS YOU'LL ALWAYS REMEMBER*

The Editors

LOVESWEPT® • 450

# Deborah Smith
# The Silver Fox and
# the Red-Hot Dove

BANTAM BOOKS
NEW YORK • TORONTO • LONDON • SYDNEY • AUCKLAND

THE SILVER FOX AND THE RED-HOT DOVE
*A Bantam Book / February 1991*

*LOVESWEPT® and the wave device are registered
trademarks of Bantam Books, a division of
Bantam Doubleday Dell Publishing Group, Inc.
Registered in U.S. Patent
and Trademark Office and elsewhere.*

*If you would be interested in receiving protective vinyl
covers for your Loveswept books, please write to this address
for information:*

Loveswept
Bantam Books
P.O. Box 985
Hicksville, NY 11802

ISBN 0-553-44074-8

*Published simultaneously in the United States and Canada*

---

*Bantam Books are published by Bantam Books, a division
of Bantam Doubleday Dell Publishing Group, Inc. Its trademark, consisting of the words "Bantam Books" and the
portrayal of a rooster, is Registered in U.S. Patent and
Trademark Office and in other countries. Marca Registrada.
Bantam Books, 666 Fifth Avenue, New York, New York 10103.*

---

PRINTED IN THE UNITED STATES OF AMERICA

OPM     0  9  8  7  6  5  4  3  2  1

# One

T. S. Audubon loved to make an entrance. He might laugh privately at his vanity, but he enjoyed the drama of his life. Richmond's magnificent old Parklane Hotel was the perfect backdrop for his unique looks, and as he crossed the lobby he knew that more eyes were on him than on its Victorian opulence. In his own way he was just as much a monument to Southern aristocracy as the hotel, and to the ladies who watched him even more awe-inspiring.

The scent of roses halted him beside a Gothic table bearing a gilded vase. A hint of the gracefulness in the movement of his long, indelicate-looking fingers, he snapped a small white rosebud from the arrangement. If he curved his fingers around a violin, they made impressive music. If he curved them around a stock portfolio, they made millions. When they stroked the trigger of a gun, they made respectful enemies. When they stroked a woman's desires, they made exquisite friends.

He tucked the rosebud into the lapel of his black tux, liking the white-on-black elegance. The white rose was the perfect accessory for his thick mane of white hair. "Good evening," he told a matronly hotel employee who had combined staring at him and walking with unfortunate results. He appreciated women who bumped into ugly rococo sofas on his behalf. "I hope you're not hurt."

"Mr. Audubon! It's so nice to see you again! Oh, no. I'm not hurt, Mr. Audubon. I'm sorry, sir. I'm so clumsy. So—"

"Please, relax. It's all right."

She twisted her hands, apparently anxious to get away from him. "The rosebud looks wonderful with your hair."

"Why, thank you. Premature gray will always be good for something, I suppose."

"Oh, yes. I didn't mean to insult you. Please, forgive me."

"I'm not insulted, I assure—"

"Oh. I'm sorry. So dense. Excuse me, sir. I have to run." Her head down, she hobbled away before he could say anything else.

Audubon's long legs took him across the lobby with an effortless speed and balance learned from years of meditative T'ai Chi and cutthroat amateur basketball. He grimaced, dismayed and distracted as he climbed the steep, central staircase. Inspiring admiration in a woman was one thing; inspiring her fearful respect was another. His grandfather had sold this hotel thirty years before, and Audubon expected to be treated as an ordinary visitor. But when seven generations of ancestors had been greedy and manipulative, when the family name was mentioned in the state's history nearly as often as Washington, Jefferson, and Lee—but with not nearly as much praise—and when a man's father was remembered as the man who destroyed the state's most beautiful tidewater marsh to build a fish-processing factory, people nominated you to the filthy rich Hall of Fame, with an emphasis on the filthy.

His mood subdued by the matronly employee's reaction, Audubon reminded himself that he was here to indulge a hobby and have a good time.

A glittering maze of people was pressing slowly through stately double doors propped open at the end of the upstairs foyer. The smell of expensive colognes and perfumes was as familiar as the scent of old money. Audubon stood back from the crowd, scanning it for familiar faces and nodding to people he recognized. Those who nodded back immediately provoked whispers from onlookers.

He knew that the gossips believed that the Audubons' only heir was adding to the family fortune by immoral, illegal means. He had lived with rumors of that kind for twenty years. And so it would always be, he assumed, because his unique work demanded secrecy.

Pulling a special invitation from an inner pocket of his tuxedo jacket, he moved through the crowd and presented it to a three-piece-suit type—undoubtedly FBI—stationed at the door to keep out any international riffraff. After all, Dr. Gregori Kriloff was Russia's leading researcher in paranormal science and one of the top five experts on the subject in the world.

"T. S. Audubon," the agent said with a slow whistle of awe under his breath. "Aren't you—"

"Just here to meet the doctor." It was not a place to talk business.

"Audubon!" A hostess from the staff of the university's administration embraced him with the enthusiasm that he, as a five-million-dollar donor, deserved. "I'll introduce you to Dr. Kriloff personally! We're about to form a receiving line, but I'm certainly not going to make *you* stand in line. Are you going to attend his lecture tomorrow?"

"I wouldn't miss it."

The woman guided him through the packed ballroom past a long table groaning with the weight of platters of delicacies. White-coated waiters hurried about with trays of glasses full of champagne, while bartenders poured liberally from bottles of vodka. Spring flowers exploded in massive arrangements set in tall urns around the room, and under a crystal chandelier a small orchestra played chamber music. Audubon searched his memory. Rachmaninoff.

Appropriately Russian—solemn, grand, filled with dark eroticism.

While his guide chattered about Russian tea, Audubon set his gaze along the line of her intended path, searching for Dr. Kriloff. The cluster of three-piece suiters with tiny lapel pins bearing the Russian flag was as subtle as the FBI man at the door.

In their center was a bearish, middle-aged man who towered above the others and wore a distinctive white tuxedo with suspenders. Someone much smaller stood beside him, hidden behind a bulky KGB agent. Audubon glimpsed the top of a honey-blond head, but nothing else.

Gregori Kriloff's height registered a good two inches above Audubon's own six feet four; his aura of command was evident in the subservient attitudes of the KGB men and the rapt attention of several university professors. He might have been Big Daddy in a Tennessee Williams's play, but his booming voice came from somewhere south of Leningrad. Audubon's attention shifted as one of the bulky KGB men stepped away from the doctor, gazing hungrily at the buffet.

For the first time, Audubon saw behind him. And almost stopped in surprise.

Dr. Kriloff's blond companion was a slender female fashion refugee so horrible looking that pity was Audubon's first reaction. She huddled in Kriloff's shadow, a notepad clutched in her pale hands, her eyes fastened firmly on the carpeted floor. Her hair was thick, straight, and raggedly chopped off at shoulder length. It was parted with all the straightness of a lightning bolt and hung in front of her glasses on one side, hiding one eye like a limp, half-shut curtain.

The glasses were large, with ugly black rims and green-tinted lenses easily a quarter-inch thick. She wore a dingy gray dress suit that belonged on a woman four sizes larger and several inches taller, though this woman was taller than average. Between the jacket's wide lapels he could see a sliver of a round-necked white blouse of some coarse material.

She never moved and never looked up. Her skirt puffed out around her skinny calves as if she were standing over an air grate, which she wasn't. And her shoes were matronly black pumps with wide heels and straps across the insteps. The woman could go hiking in those shoes.

"Who is she?" Audubon put a hand on his hostess's arm and brought them to a stop a dozen feet from the Kriloff group. "The blonde."

"His secretary." The hostess covered her mouth and whispered sideways, "Isn't she awful looking? That gray bag makes her into a skinny-legged pigeon. Why in the world would Dr. Kriloff allow a member of his entourage to make such a terrible impression? People can barely keep from gawking at her. Thank goodness, she doesn't speak English. At least she won't be hurt if she overhears a critical remark."

"Introduce me to her." Audubon drew the hostess forward, ignoring her disbelieving stare. Part of his intention was based on sympathy, part on curiosity, and part on a personal challenge to thumb his nose at every blue blood who was cruel to this pitiful red pigeon. *Pigeon.* It was really an insult to the bird.

As the hostess introduced Audubon to Dr. Kriloff, he caught the blond pigeon giving him furtive glances from behind the glasses and the shaggy screen of hair. Immediately she ducked her head and stared at the floor again.

Audubon was excellent at aiming his concentration in several directions at once; it was a survival trait learned in Vietnam and honed over the eighteen years since. But his Russian was elementary and required too much thought; for the moment he could only converse with Kriloff, telling him that he was in the import/export business—which was basically true—and that his interest in paranormal studies dated back to his mother, who had claimed to be psychic.

"Very interesting," the doctor said, looking bored.

"You come to hear me speak, tomorrow. It was nice to meet you."

Audubon had never cared whether Kriloff was likable or not; he was interested only in the man's research, what little of it was known—only tidbits of Kriloff's research reached the outside world. Audubon figured there were dozens of secret projects the scientist was working on.

However, Audubon couldn't stomach the way the man ignored the pigeon, keeping his back turned to her. The pigeon seemed to be shrinking quickly. Action was needed before her clothes swallowed her and she disappeared into a heap of them on the carpet.

The hostess responded to the message in Audubon's slight nod. "Dr. Kriloff, I'm afraid my Russian is nonexistent. Mr. Audubon has asked me to introduce him to Miss Petrovic. Would you do the honors, since she doesn't speak English?"

Kriloff's meager charm disappeared completely. He scowled at Audubon and studied him shrewdly. With obvious reluctance he turned toward the slender woman. She slightly tilted up her head and gazed at Kriloff from under her brows. Getting a little better look at her face, Audubon noted the sharply rising color in her cheeks, the lovely complexion beneath them, the sweep of a graceful neck, and the hard chin kept in submission by soft, pretty lips that were clamped into a neutral line.

It wasn't a terribly homely face, he saw, and could have been considerably improved by some work on the terrible hair and a better pair of glasses. He couldn't see her eyes well, especially from his side view, but what he saw magnified his interest a thousand percent. For all her apparent timidity, the eyelashes behind the glasses didn't flutter while she listened intently to Dr. Kriloff. Her posture was meek, but the eyes peering up at Kriloff were only pretending at it.

"Elena, meet Mr. Audubon," Kriloff said in curt

Russian. "He does not use a first name. Mr. Audubon, meet my assistant, Elena Petrovic."

Something subtle passed between Kriloff and the woman, something Audubon deciphered as a warning. She lowered her eyes again, swung her head toward Audubon, and without looking at him said, *"Zdrahstvuyti,"* in a soft, throaty voice. It stirred something warm and deep inside him, and to his amazement the warmth became a slight throbbing in his blood. He had never judged any woman's sensuality by her looks, but Elena Petrovic's determined frumpiness stretched his limits. Again he heard the erotic voice, melting into his ears.

*"Zdrahstvuyti, Mystyer Audubon."*

He snapped out of his trance and smiled at her—or at least at her bowed head. *"Zdrahstvuyti, Elena."*

"Excuse us, now, Mr. Audubon," Kriloff interjected. "I believe I am to meet the other guests in a receiving line. Good-bye." He motioned for Elena Petrovic to follow him, snapping blunt fingers under her downcast eyes.

"Would you like to dance, Elena?" Audubon said quickly, his Russian clumsy but effective. Her gaze shot up to his. The eyes behind the tinted glasses were wide, light globes of undeterminable color, but brilliant with life, intelligence, shock—and hope. They shot downward again just as quickly.

Her fate, as far as Audubon was concerned, was sealed. She was a caldron of mystery, and nothing short of an international scene would keep him from taking her away from Dr. Kriloff, at least temporarily.

"She does not dance," Kriloff said.

Audubon stepped forward, politely but oh-so-firmly inserting all two hundred and twenty pounds of his tall body into hers and Kriloff's path. "The music is very slow. It would be easy to teach her. Please. I'd like to have a chance to improve my Russian, and I'm sure Elena can help."

The doctor stiffened with aggravation. "She does not dance. She does not speak English. She is very shy. Excuse us."

From under the sheet of lank blond hair came carefully submissive Russian, almost a whisper. "Please, I would like to learn to dance, Doctor. This is our last week in America, after all."

Audubon watched, intrigued but growing angrier, as Dr. Kriloff glared at her. He sensed that he was seeing a battle of wills that had been brewing for a long time. Was she this stern patriarch's lover? Didn't he have a wife and daughter somewhere, mentioned in an article? Was this jealousy on his part, or something more complicated?

Whatever it was, her situation ignited Audubon's compassion and desire to help the helpless, a desire that had fostered his ideals, his work, his life. He thought acidly that Kriloff had started a war and didn't know it.

"Dance, if you want," Kriloff allowed finally. His heavy face regained its composure, but with an obvious effort. "It is, after all, our last week here. You should have a little freedom."

"Yes, thank you," she said, twisting her notepad in her hands. Abruptly she pivoted and gave it to one of the men in their entourage. Then she faced Audubon, managed to raise her eyes to the pearl buttons on his pleated shirtfront, and simply waited.

"I'm honored," he said, groaning inwardly because the limits of his Russian were going to make an intimate conversation impossible. Why couldn't she be French, Spanish, German, Italian, or even Greek? He had fluently charmed women in all of those languages.

But body language was universal. He held out a hand, palm up, and she stared at it for a second. Then she slipped her pale, cool-looking hand across his palm and curled her fingers gently around his. The pale hand wasn't cool at all, but deliciously warm in a way he'd never felt before, almost hot, and until he shook the strange idea off, he thought that she was communicating desire to him through channels of energy that went far beyond the ordinary thrill of touch.

"Enjoy yourself, Elena," Dr. Kriloff said sharply, and walked away. She gave a jerky nod in response, her gaze fastened on Audubon's hand as if it were the most enticing object her lowered eyes had ever beheld.

And he stood there, forty years old, a veteran of seductions he had always controlled, and felt helplessly enchanted by a woman who was shy, plain, laughably dressed, and incapable of communicating in his own language.

Gently he led her to a small teak parquet dance floor in front of the orchestra. Everyone else was in line to meet Kriloff; the floor was empty, the chamber music wrong for dancing, and Elena Petrovic looked even more out of place under the glittering chandelier. She kept glancing at Kriloff with obvious worry.

"Am I bothering you? To dance?" Audubon asked in his inept Russian, facing her as they came to a stop. *"Embarrassing you,"* he added in English, as if it might help. "I don't mean to."

"Bother? No," she answered in Russian. "I will dance with you no matter what anyone else wishes. You're special."

She said it without coyness, as if it were simply something she had recognized and accepted immediately. Her voice made goose bumps rise on his flesh. He was enormously pleased at the same time that his sophistication shrugged off her flattery. He looked down at their joined hands, surprised to feel her hand trembling. He was shocked to realize within seconds that it was only his imagination, because what he felt was the fascinating, invisible vibration again, as if she'd surrounded him with an aura of welcome.

"You've been touring America for two months. Am I the first American who tried to speak with you?" he asked gruffly.

"The first who didn't give up quickly. No one has ever made Dr. Kriloff uncomfortable before. I could tell from the tone of his voice that he finds you threatening, even though you're a stranger. You have a sense of your own importance. People watch you, to see what you'll do next." She added grimly, "Now they are watching me, too, unfortunately."

"Then we'll shock them together."

"I know I'm ugly. I don't mind, if you don't."

"You're not ugly." *The most gallant lie I ever told.* She held up her other hand, found his with a sureness that seemed to come like an inner radar, and warmed him again with perplexing ideas about communication and desire. *She's not ugly,* he concluded, and it was a staggering leap of faith, but no lie.

"You are a kind liar, Mr. Audubon, and you like to cause trouble. Is that why you asked me to dance?"

"After you talked my ears off and threw yourself into my arms, what else could I do?"

Her startled gasp became a soft, musical chuckle. The light from the chandelier flickered on her glowing cheeks. The reaction of his appreciative masculine impulses signaled she had just redefined *ugly* once and for all.

His next step brought his torso close enough to touch her floppy jacket lapels. The top of her head was level with his nose, and the lanky hair had a clean, sweet scent that made him forget its looks. She stared fixedly downward, as if hypnotized by his pleats, pearls, and the rosebud boutonniere. "When I remember America, I'll remember tonight most of all," she told him. "Meeting you . . . I mean, being asked to dance by such an interesting American is worth everything."

"We move like this," he told her in Russian. "Only a little. We can't do anything important to this music." *If we were in bed we could, but that's a different dance.*

"Important?" she asked.

He searched for a clearer word and sighed with exasperation. Muttering under his breath in English, a distracted part of his mind noted that she was swaying with him more gracefully than he'd expected. In fact, when he put one hand against the small of her back, she came alive like a willow, and he felt as if she were bending against his palm.

Then he realized he'd been thinking out loud, saying *flexible*, but in English. Audubon tucked his chin and studied the camouflaged face behind the glasses and hair. "Do you speak *any* English?"

"No." She darted a glance toward the receiving line and Audubon's gaze followed. Kriloff looked up from shaking hands to glare at them. "No," she repeated firmly.

Audubon took in the exchange with great satisfaction. *She speaks English.* But why would Kriloff be so determined to keep her quiet?

"I speak such bad Russian," Audubon told her, sighing. "I give up. Talk to me. Tell me about yourself, and I'll try to translate."

Her hand curled more tightly around his. She had rested her other hand on his shoulder; now it crept higher and slipped around his neck. He could tell exactly where her fingertips were, even through his jacket. It was odd—they made tantalizing hot spots at the top of his spine. The nagging twinge from an old muscle pull faded magically. What seductive distraction!

"I cannot talk to you very much," she whispered, her eyes still lowered. "It wouldn't be wise. You talk to me."

"Why are you afraid?"

Her hand cooled inside his. The heat of her fingertips disappeared. "I cannot," she repeated, sounding angry and sad.

"Are you afraid of Dr. Kriloff?"

"I'll have to leave if you don't stop asking me questions like that, Mr. Audubon."

"No, don't leave. I'll talk to you in English, even if you don't understand. I like to talk."

"I noticed. Good. I like your voice, *Rhett Butler.*"

He chuckled. Her hands warmed again. The startling temperature changes, the sway in her body, the lithe feel of it, and the feminine scent of her hair made him giddy. He tried to remember the last time *giddy* had described anything about his emotions, and concluded that he had probably been in grammar school. "All right, English it is, then. Here goes." He cleared his throat dramatically, and one corner of her mouth drew up in amusement. It was the only sign that she was listening, as her downcast eyes continued to explore his shirtfront.

"You're the most unique woman I've ever met, and I suspect you're hiding a great deal about yourself."

Her expression was as unchanging as the Siberian tundra, but there was a tiny quiver in the upturned corner of her mouth.

"You remind me of a pigeon that's had its wings clipped, Elena."

The orchestra's strings swelled to a throbbing, plaintive melody. She and he were barely moving, the dance a pretense for closeness. A nervous patter of Russian burst from her. "When I was a little girl, I saw a silver fox outside my bedroom window one night. You remind me of him, with your white hair. I used to make up stories about him. I *thought* I could trust him."

"If you'd speak English, we could discuss your fantasies about me in greater detail."

"I *wish* I knew what you were saying. Anyhow, silver foxes are very rare. Sometimes I wonder if I didn't just *imagine* I saw one. He never came back after that night. Foxes may be handsome and smart, but they aren't very reliable, are they? Even the most unusual ones."

"I *wish* I knew what you were saying," he mimicked. "Something about wanting a silver fox to visit your bedroom at night?"

"This is a very strange conversation. Anyone who was watching wouldn't guess we're speaking different languages. They would even think I understand what you're saying."

"You do. What little I can see of your face is scarlet. And believe me, Rhett knows what scarlet means."

"Here are simple questions you can answer in Russian. How old are you? Are you married?"

*"Sohrak. Nyet."* He continued casually, but in English, "Although I'm forty years old and have never been married, I've enjoyed the company of several wonderful women. I'm a connoisseur, you see, and connoisseurs need variety." He chuckled at his excuses then lowered his voice to a brocaded, teasing drawl. "I've never met anyone quite like you, though. I think you agree, even if you *don't* understand English, that we could improve international relations immensely if we were alone in a private room right now."

Her stoic facade never cracked. "How old am I? I'm twenty-nine."

"After we made love, we'd lay close together and talk. I'd run one hand over you very slowly while I told you about myself. Then you could return the favor."

Russian ice. "Here's another question you should understand in my language. What is your first name?"

"You'll have to make love to me if you want to find out. I've never told anyone, but I'd tell *you.*"

"Why don't you answer in Russian, so I can understand you?"

"You understand me." He stopped moving and held her still.

"I have to go. Good-bye."

He brought one hand up swiftly, hooked a forefinger under her glasses, and swept them into his hand in one neat move. Her head jerked up and she made a startled sound, then looked around quickly to see if Dr. Kriloff was watching. He was. *"Pazhahlasta!"*

He held the lenses up for scrutiny and nodded. "Fakes. This pigeon has terrible taste in glasses but excellent eyesight."

*"Pazhahlasta,"* she begged again, her voice trembling.

Audubon rebuked himself for complicating her unpleasant situation. "I apologize, Elena. Here." He slipped the glasses back into place, pushing her half curtain of hair aside with his fingertip. He caught his breath at the full sight of her strained, upturned face. The strength and balance of cool, unadorned porcelain presented themselves as a backdrop for a tempting but disciplined mouth and light blue eyes under the dramatic wings of coppery brows.

Those eyes, covered with the awful glasses once more, troubled him. He'd seen trapped, wary hope too often not to recognize it in her searing gaze. "If you want to stay in America, I'll help you," he whispered.

He still held one of her hands as he had while they were dancing, but the wonderful warmth was gone. She stiffened, withdrawing. "I do not understand English." It was an angry, mechanical defense.

"I'm not with the government—either yours or ours. This isn't a trick. I enjoy helping people in, uhmmm, *problem* situations."

"Speak Russian!"

"I want to help you. I think you want my help. Here." Turning her so that Kriloff's view of their hands was obscured, he slipped a hand inside his jacket and quickly produced a pale gold business card bearing only a phone number. Pulling her close and smiling pleasantly for anyone who might be watching, he brushed his mouth over hers while his hand darted inside her jacket. Deftly his fingers slid between the plain white buttons on the front of her blouse and tucked the business card between her bra and the luxurious swell of a breast.

Just as quickly he stepped back, feeling confident, aroused—and worried. She looked shocked and upset, her chest rising and falling swiftly. The magnetic blue eyes stared at him, analyzing and assessing. Her hand rose to her throat, fumbled, grasped the front of her blouse over the spot where he'd inserted his fingers, then flattened. She looked to Audubon like a kid in grammar school who was trying to find her heart for the pledge of allegiance.

Audubon sensed the KGB agent before the man stepped between them, nodding to Elena Petrovic and speaking in low, urgent tones. She shuddered visibly and looked toward Kriloff. Her hands fell to her sides. Her head sank and she leveled her gaze at the carpet again, becoming the meek pigeon from before.

Audubon fought a reckless desire to snatch her away, no matter what the consequences. It was possible he'd made a mistake in judging her, but he was willing to take that chance. He stepped forward, began to raise his hand, then halted.

How could he risk a scandal that would endanger his work, as well as all the people who worked for him? Raging inside, he forced his face into a pleasant expression. He would have to find a way to help her that was not immediately confrontational . . . or perhaps even obvious.

"*Da svidahniya, Mystyer Audubon,*" she said in a subdued voice.

"Good night, Elena."

The man escorted her across the ballroom and out the doors. Kriloff still stood at the head of the receiving line, pumping hands and glaring over people's heads. Audubon met his challenge with a cold smile, letting seven generations of blue-blooded patrician arrogance rise to the surface to help make his point.

He wondered what the crowd's gossips were whispering about this scene. Then he laughed at their overt stares and plucked the boutonniere from his lapel, jauntily twirling it by the stem as he walked from the dance floor. The silky petals brushed the tops of his fingertips, and he looked down in surprise. "What the hell?" he asked out loud, and stopped in his tracks.

The tightly furled little rose bud was now in glorious full bloom.

"You shouldn't have done that." Sergei moaned, wringing his big hands as he walked down the hall with Elena. "Now we probably won't be allowed to go shopping for souvenirs tomorrow. You'll be confined to your room until we leave for home!"

Sergei was as fussy as a grandmother. When she was little, Elena had even called him *babushka*, to his chagrin. Ordinarily she would have patted his arm in sympathy, but she was in a daze over the amazing Mr. Audubon.

His card lay smoothly against the top of her left breast, as if his fingers still coaxed her with their secretive, rebellious, and probably deceptive touch. Who was he, really? *What* was he? The Americans had spies and agents everywhere, according to Sergei. And Kriloff had warned her repeatedly not to trust anyone they met in the United States. Because she'd been sheltered from outside news and information all of her life, she could only believe what she was told.

She clenched her fists and wanted to scream from a lifetime of frustration. It was maddening to be kept so ignorant and helpless. Even a hostile American world was better than a future without even a taste of freedom. Back at home, Kriloff's newest research project was waiting for her. She'd rather die than return to *that*. The two-month American lecture tour was almost over, and her chances of escape were dwindling. All of the groveling she'd done to win her place on this trip would be for nothing!

Elena looked around the hallway desperately. With Sergei beside her every minute of the day and another bodyguard by her door every night, she had no opportunities. She'd been such a fool to jeopardize everything by dancing with the American!

"Why did you do it?" Sergei asked, as he lumbered ahead of her and punched the elevator button. "Why did you let that smug American cause trouble for you?"

Elena stared hollow-eyed at her humiliating gray image in the mirrorlike surface of the elevator doors. *I couldn't help myself. He was wonderful.* "I'm a grown woman who has never been asked to dance before." She raised knotted fists and begged, "Sergei, why should I live like this? No one should live this way. I want to be treated like an adult. Like an ordinary woman."

"You had Pavel. He didn't treat you like a child."

The shame and fury that rose inside her made poor Sergei look guilty and nervously stroke his thinning gray hair. He'd made a mistake by bringing up the most painful reminder of Kriloff's manipulation. In a low, trembling voice Elena said, "Mr. Audubon wasn't *hired* to service my romantic needs. He offered of his own accord. Forgive me, but I was overwhelmed by the novelty of it."

"Oh, Laney-kitten, I'm sorry to see you so unhappy. I understand, really. But we must do our duty—"

"I've been dutiful all my life!" She looked around again, then grasped his hands. "Please, Sergei, help me live a real life, like everyone else."

The elevator arrived and the door began to open. Sergei put an arm around her shoulders and hugged her awkwardly. "To your room now, Laney-kitten. No more rebellious talk."

She stared into the elevator's shining hull. It was a casket. If she went inside, she'd be burying herself and her dreams. *Call Mr. Audubon tomorrow.* No. He must be a trickster. American men were self-serving playboys, weren't they? She couldn't trust him any more than she'd trusted her childhood faith in fairy tales.

"What's wrong, Laney-kitten?" Sergei tugged on her elbow. "Come along. Into the elevator with you."

Oh, she was going crazy, caught in T. S. Audubon's spell. She'd seen a silver fox outside her window at the institute one night more than twenty-five years ago. The stories she'd dreamed up about him rescuing her had only been a child's way to battle grief and loneliness. Why did they pull at her memory now? *Because he's finally come back to help you.*

"Elena!" Sergei was angry and worried now. He pushed her forward gently, but with a firm grip. She dug her heels into the hallway's Turkish carpet. All was lost, but she had to fight. Even futile rebellion was better than meek captivity. "Elena, I'll have to report this!"

His next sentence was drowned out by the sudden shrieking of alarm systems. Elena clamped her hands over her ears. Down the hall, people hurried from the ballroom. "What is it?" she yelled to Sergei.

"Fire alarms! Stay here! Right here! I'll be back!" He galloped toward the crowd. Elena gaped at his retreating bulk. Could it be possible? The alarm seemed to be screaming inside her head. *Now! Run!* She pivoted blindly, searching. Beyond the elevators was a door marked Emergency Exit.

Five seconds later she was headed down a stark, concrete stairwell, her feet racing to catch up with her heart.

When the alarms sounded, Audubon skirted the panicky crowd with a calmness borne of his work's routine brushes with chaos. He managed to get out before the throng of people completely blocked his way. Elena Petrovic's stocky, aging bodyguard rushed toward him, headed back into the ballroom. Audubon grabbed his arm. "Where is Miss Petrovic?"

"Waiting by the elevators!"

As the man continued past, Audubon's shrewd gaze shot to the elevators. Elena Petrovic was gone. Beyond the elevators the emergency door to the stairwell was swinging closed. Audubon glimpsed an unmistakable flash of gray. So the pigeon had flown the coop.

The crowd surged out and surrounded him. He cursed eloquently under his breath as he dodged around people. By the time he reached the stairwell, he could only hear the faint patter of feet below him. When he reached the basement parking garage, he swung toward the unmanned exit booth and saw her running past it toward the darkness of a deserted city street. The sheer beauty of her long-legged stride made him want to cheer; her speed made him groan with dismay.

He reached the street in time to see her run into a nearby intersection between tall office buildings. A lone pickup truck with a covered bed idled at a red light, unsuspecting. She made a beeline for it, pulled up the canvas flap emblazoned Nilly's Fine Vegetables, Artemis Island, VA, and climbed inside the truck's tall, wooden shed.

Audubon memorized the license plate just as the light changed. He stood in the center of the street, watching the truck pull away, feeling triumphant but sorry for her, because she'd had to resort to such a pitiful avenue for escape. The flap lifted at one corner. She peeked out and froze when she saw him. Then the flap snapped down again.

Audubon strolled back inside the hotel where security guards were yelling that everything was all right, that someone had pulled the alarm as a prank. Humming under his breath, he went to a phone in the lobby and called his estate. Within fifteen minutes his elite network was preparing to track the flight of the fascinating, mysterious, and possibly dangerous pigeon, whom Audubon intended to capture for himself.

# Two

"So you really can't talk?"

Elena nodded her head again and stared at the sun rising over the ocean to her right. She was exhausted, frightened, and trying hard to think of a plan. Her indecision focused on T. S. Audubon for the hundredth time. What had he been up to last night? Who had he told about her escape route? Bitter sorrow filled her as she considered the possibility that her silver fox might just be a silver rat. *Her silver fox.* He had made his mark on her imagination forever.

An hour before, Beckel Nilly had discovered her in the back of his truck during a stop to buy fuel. Elena had been certain her escape attempt was finished. There were so many criminals in America, Sergei had said, that no one trusted strangers. So who would help a Russian found huddled among tomato crates without money, luggage, or identification?

But the woman had only grunted with mild surprise and peered at her as if she were an interesting new type of vegetable. "If you're a runnin' from somebody," Beckel Nilly had said, "you might as well do it up front in the cab."

Shocked, Elena had realized all wasn't lost. But her voice, her accent—how could she get by without revealing it? She pointed to her throat and shook her head.

"Can't talk? Won't talk? Here." Beckel had pulled a grimy notepad from a pocket of her work shirt and thrust it into Elena's hands. "Can you write?" Elena gave her a fervent nod and quickly put down, *I am honest person. Please forgive intrusion. I can hear but cannot talk. Am running away from home.*

A home half a world away, but that was beside the point.

"Where's home?"

Elena searched her knowledge of America for a safe lie. *Chevrolet.*

"A car?"

Elena groaned at her error. *A town in the next state,* she wrote.

"What's your name?"

She thought furiously, trying to come up with something that sounded very American. *Madonna Sinatra.*

"Where're you headed?"

Elena shrugged. She had no idea.

"Need a job? If you can hoe weeds, pick vegetables, and clean house, you can stay with me. I live on an island. You can't crave company, and work for me, I warn ya. It's a lonely place. You'll get about ten dollars a week, plus room and board. You want the job or not?"

Maybe this woman was a little crazy, but she didn't seem devious. At least she wasn't going to turn Elena over to the police. All Elena had to do was act like an American and keep out of sight on Beckel Nilly's island, then.

"Ain't got all day," Beckel Nilly said. "You want the job or not?"

She would hide with this odd woman and learn how to act like an American while she decided what to do next. She hoped that T. S. Audubon wouldn't look for her. She suspected he would. She scribbled out an answer. *Okay.*

*   *   *

"I'm going in on the south side, where the woods are. Give me that map report again." Audubon lounged in the captain's chair, guiding the boat with one hand and holding the radio mike with the other. Artemis Island loomed ahead, looking like any other coastal island, a green-blue mound of forest rimmed with beach. One of his helicopters passed over it lazily like a harmless, oversized bee.

"Audubon? The house is about a half mile from the south beach. There's a trail through the woods. And—wait! I see her. She's walking in from the field. I think I've spooked her. She keeps looking up."

"Leave. *Now.* I'll call you as soon as I get back to the boat with her."

"Okay, boss. Out."

Audubon put the mike aside and straightened in the chair. His heart was pounding with excitement. He tossed a dirty blue baseball cap, with its fish hook decorations, aside, then smiled at his torn sneakers, grimy brown trousers, and sweat-stained shirt. Acting the part of a derelict fisherman had been the perfect way to win Beckel Nilly's friendship. When he'd helped her load her truck on the mainland docks, she'd told him all about her new worker.

Audubon threw his head back and laughed. He gave "Madonna Sinatra" points for creativity. His laughter fading, he thought she also deserved points for courage and resourcefulness.

Not that any of those qualities would help her to elude him. Since Beckel Nilly was on her way to Richmond with a load of vegetables, Ms. Petrovic-Sinatra, alone and unsuspecting on the island coming up close on his starboard, was ripe for picking.


Elena paced the creaking wooden floor of Beckel Nilly's living room, her bare feet making worried little squeaks. She took deep breaths of the breeze that curled through every corner of the clapboard house. She wrung the sides of her shapeless, sleeveless dress of brightly flowered cotton. It was made from a seed sack, and Beckel Nilly had given it to her, saying it had become too small for her to wear ten years ago.

When the helicopter flew over her in the vegetable field, Elena had wanted to duck inside the dress and hide. She was terrified that someone had found her. Now, going to one corner of the ramshackle room, she picked up a deadly little harpoon gun and studied it anxiously. The razor-sharp arrow protruding from the end of the barrel made her flinch at the thought of what it could do. Mrs. Nilly had taught her how to shoot the device, and Elena was convinced then that Americans were, indeed, very worried about crime.

When she heard steps on the back porch, she moaned under her breath, and, leveling the harpoon gun in front of her, went down a hallway strewn with farm tools.

Slow footsteps crossed the porch and entered the kitchen through the warped screen door. She halted, trembling, her ears alert to catch the sound of the slightest movement. But there were no more sounds. She squinted in the bright light filling the end of the hallway from a large window that faced the western sky.

When T. S. Audubon stepped silently into the hall, she jumped. He was barefoot. He stopped, legs apart, hands hanging calmly by his sides, the window's light turning him into an unnerving masculine silhouette of power and drama. "I'm not here to hurt you, Elena." He spoke in English, his voice low and coaxing. "I know you're here alone, but you don't have to be afraid of me. I've come to take you to a safe place."

The liquid richness of his voice played on her cold skin, but she was certain now that he worked for his government. What ordinary citizen would have followed her so diligently and known how to spy on Mrs. Nilly's schedule? "Get out," she commanded. "I'm not leaving this island."

"You speak excellent English, even when you're upset. I'm glad you can understand me. And I know you can see me, even if you're not wearing your fake glasses. Now, listen. I can help you."

"Why?"

"I enjoy helping people."

"Why?"

"Explaining would take longer than you'd like. But if you want to stay in the United States, you're going about it the wrong way. I can change that."

"I just want to be free. I don't need your help." She clutched the harpoon. "I'm only a secretary. What do you want with me?"

"Tell me why you're so important to Kriloff. He accused me of stealing you. He's causing an uproar with our State Department. I don't think the loss of a secretary would be worth an ugly break in diplomacy. Do you?"

"I will find help on my own. I don't trust you."

"You trusted me the other night. You wanted to be as close to me as you could get."

"A dance. The spell of the music. We Russians are warm-blooded and impetuous. It meant nothing."

"I've danced with a lot of women. The communication between you and me was not nothing."

"I won't go back! I'm hurting no one! Why can't all of you let me alone?"

"Why are you so important to Dr. Kriloff? Are you his lover?"

The breath burst from her in a yelp of disgust. "No! He has a wife and daughter in Moscow! And I would *never* let him—oh! What a dreadful thing to suspect of me! Do you think I'm so ugly that I'd—oh!"

"Hmmm. Why does he treat you like a slave?"

"Because I *was* a slave! But now I'm free! And I'll never cooperate with anyone again! I'd rather die!"

The silhouette's hands, raised in gentle supplication, struck a deep chord in her. "You don't have to die," T. S. Audubon said with a kindness that added to her confusion. "I'll take you to my home. You'll be safe there."

A new thought chilled her. She had never had much contact with the world outside Kriloff's institute, and therefore little experience with the motivations of men, either Russian or American. She couldn't begin to fathom the enigmatic Audubon's interest in her, but she had been treated to a terrible lesson in men's motivations by Pavel. "If you're not with the government, and you don't want to give me back to my own people, then there is only one reason you came to capture me. For sex!"

He coughed, caught a sound deep in his throat, and suddenly she realized he was suppressing a laugh. He looked toward heaven. "A dirty, skinny, shaggy-haired, weapon-toting woman in a brightly flowered seed sack is accusing me of lecherous intentions." His gaze shifted to her again. "I assure you, madame, I prefer my women well-groomed, unarmed, and wearing something that doesn't have 'Dutch Girl Alfalfa' stenciled across the bottom."

His teasing made her burn with humiliation. "So you were not telling the truth the other night. I *am* ugly to you. Good. Then you don't have any reason to want me. Go away. I've never done anything bad to you."

"Except refuse my help." The kindness returned to his voice. "Look, I'm in the import/export business. I consider helping you a work-related challenge. You might say you're the most interesting import I've run across in a long time."

"I can't trust you or anyone else! I've waited too long for this chance. All I'm asking you to do is leave and not tell anyone that you know where I am. Please. *Please.* It means my whole future, my life, because I *will die* rather than return home with Kriloff."

"What has he done to you?" Audubon asked in a grim, low tone.

"I don't want to discuss my life with you."

"A person as desperate as you are has been tortured in some way—if not physically, then emotionally. Come with me, Elena. I'll never let that bastard hurt you again. I swear it."

The edge in his voice was so new and so lethal, it frightened rather than reassured her. Americans were barbaric and bloodthirsty, Sergei said. The richest among them lived like mobsters, ordering terrible revenges on people who displeased them. What if she did something that upset this supremely powerful and authoritative man?

Her knees were weak, but she forced herself to move. Backing up by slow degrees, she kept the harpoon gun pointed at the spot where his chest flowed into an athlete's waist. His shirt hung open down the center, giving her a bold target of masculine hair and muscle.

Once, as part of her performances for Kriloff's important friends, she'd healed a famous Lithuanian weight lifter who suffered from liver trouble. His stomach had felt like T. S. Audubon's looked. She couldn't picture that wall of hard flesh letting even a harpoon arrow through . . . and the mere thought of hurting him made her nauseous.

"Put down the gun," he coaxed. "I won't make a move. I promise."

"I *want* you to move. Go back where you came from."

"My family came over from France about two hundred and twenty years ago. I think it's too late to go back. I know you'll trust me as soon as we have a chance to talk. I have a boat waiting just offshore. Time is precious. I'm very good at what I do, but it's quite possible your belligerent comrades have managed to follow me."

"So *that's* your plan. We'll reach the mainland, and they'll be there, waiting, and you can say it wasn't your fault! *No!*" She started to pivot and run, but she'd backed too close to the side of the hallway, and her elbow slammed into the wall.

The harpoon gun jerked, recoiled, and released its arrow with an ominous hissing sound. The arrow hit Audubon in the right side, sinking deeply into a spot under his rib cage.

Elena dropped the gun and covered her horrified

scream with both hands. He staggered, clasped a hand around the arrow's steel shaft, and groaned with pain as he worked it loose. He dropped the arrow and pressed his hand over the wound. Blood poured through his fingers.

"Wouldn't happen to have a Band-Aid, would you?" he said with an amazing attempt at a smile through clenched teeth. She took several numb steps forward, gazing at him in anguish. He squinted at her in obvious agony.

"I didn't mean to do it," she whispered.

"Is there a radio here?"

"It's broken. Mrs. Nilly was supposed to pick up a new transistor today."

He looked down at the cascade of blood that now stained the bottom half of his shirt. Then he left the hall and walked swiftly through the kitchen, taking a hand towel from the sink to plaster against the terrible wound, and hunching over with pain. Elena followed him in tormented silence. "Call my people, the first chance you get," he urged, his voice a rasp. "Use the card . . . I gave you. May be your only . . . hope."

With impressive strength and determination he left the house and strode between the clumps of saw grass in the sandy backyard. Her conscience on fire, Elena stood on the porch steps and stared after him as he disappeared down the trail under a dense canopy of moss-draped trees.

Her guilt warred with self-preservation. He'd be all right. He'd go to his boat and call for help. She'd have time to take Mrs. Nilly's little fishing skiff and leave from the opposite side of the island. She couldn't risk her future for him. He wasn't going to die if she didn't help him.

She sank to the steps and sat there for several minutes, her hands knotted into fists of emotion against her face. Even from the porch she could see where his blood had spattered the sand. A fierce, unrelenting thought tore at her. *The arrow hit an artery. He may bleed to death before his people can reach him.*

Her fingers burned with energy. Every instinct that flowed from her gift urged her to do what she was meant to do, to use the wonderful power that had never been perverted, not even by Kriloff. Crying, she shook her fists and looked toward heaven. "All I wanted was to be free!"

She leapt from the steps and ran after Audubon.

He woke with his head in someone's lap and his legs in the ocean. A shadow made his face feel cooler than his arms. He could feel the sun on them as well as on his bare chest and stomach. He could feel the softness of the thighs beneath his head. He could feel the strange, tingling heat against his side.

It was all very pleasurable, and suddenly he realized that none of it would have felt so good if he were dead. He opened his eyes quickly and stared up into the faded cotton flowers covering Elena Petrovic's chest. She was bent over him so deeply that he inhaled the soap-fresh scent of the fabric and the sexual, feminine scent of her body. With ease he could have lifted his head and nuzzled the mounds that pressed downward against the thin cloth. Hibiscus had never looked so interesting before.

He was in a languid mood, as if half-asleep. Slowly he tried to remember how he'd gotten this way. His last memory was of sinking to his knees in the surf, too weak and dizzy to climb into the dinghy he'd left on shore. It had floated away, taking his last bit of consciousness with it.

Now energy was flowing back into him through the puzzling sensation beneath his rib cage. The wound! He tilted his head up in a hurry to see what was happening, but instead mashed his upper face into the lovely upside-down hills covered in hibiscus.

Elena leaned back, taking her shadow with her. Sunshine flooded his eyes and he turned his head to one side, blinking, his mind and eyes beginning to focus. He disliked the helpless feeling, which reminded him of the time he'd been wounded in Vietnam. But when Elena ran her hands up his chest, bringing the comforting, energized glow with them, he exhaled with delight.

Her hands flattened over the center of his chest; his heart seemed to be drawn to them, to her. He was liquid inside, responding to the pull of her elements. It was like nothing he'd felt before, like nothing any other woman had made him feel . . . or want. "What are you doing to me?" he asked.

"I applied pressure to your wound." Her voice sounded drained, hollow. "Nothing mysterious. It stopped the bleeding. Sheer luck." Her hands fell from his chest, cupped his head, then lowered it to the sand as she slid from under him.

Audubon raised up on his elbow and looked at himself. The surf ruffled over his lower legs, taking away red clouds of blood that had soaked his trousers on the side beneath his wound. His shirt hung open, the ends trailing red streamers on the sand. His torso's covering of fine, dark brown hair, which had never turned white like the hair on his head, was crusted with dried blood.

He'd come much closer to dying than he'd realized. Elena Petrovic had stopped the bleeding with simple pressure techniques? Impossible. Quickly he craned his head so that he could find the wound under his rib cage. Shock poured through him. The gash was dry, and the edges had closed. They were already forming pink ridges of scar tissue.

He stared in utter disbelief, then rubbed his eyes and looked again. Cool air from the surf misted him, and he shivered. Probing the wound with his fingertips, he expected it to change back into what he *knew* it should be. It didn't.

Audubon shot upright, peeled his shirt off, and explored the area around the wound again and again, frowning. He'd led a highly adventurous life that had left him immune to feelings of wonder. Now his cynicism was washed away by wide-eyed fascination, and he felt like a child who believed in magic.

From the corner of his eye he caught Elena's movement and swiveled to watch her. She was a short distance away, curled up on her side in the sand above the surf line. She had one arm under her head as a pillow. Loose chunks of blond hair, matted by the wind and moisture, fell over her exhausted-looking face, and she observed him through it with sad, groggy eyes.

When he vaulted toward her, she frowned and started to push herself upright, but appeared too weary to fight. Audubon knelt beside her, slid a hand under the ragged cascade of hair, traced the lines of the smooth, slender neck, and found the pulse point under her jaw. Her pulse felt strong but a little fast—no surprise, since she was obviously afraid of him. But what else was wrong with her?

"Are you sick?" he asked.

"No. Just exhausted." She braced herself with both arms. Her head drooped. "Exhausted, and angry, and defeated. Caught in my own trap, you might say."

"What did you do to my wound? How did you heal it?"

"Forget your questions, Mr. Audubon. I won't answer them. I don't care what happens to me. I won't cooperate."

He was bewildered, excited, and alarmed by her mystery. The sorrow and resignation in her voice filled him with sympathy, but the practical part of him said now was the time to take this valuable prize home for further study. He had earned his reputation for unsentimental idealism. Others might picture him as a bit driven and manipulative, but they never complained about his motives.

Then his practical self faltered, still dazed by the miracle she'd created with her hands. "You saved my life," he murmured. "There's no explanation for how you did it. I should be dead. Without your talent for miracles, I would be. I feel . . . I feel like one of those people who have near-death experiences and come back to consciousness knowing that their lives will never be the same."

"You're overreacting. I told you, I just applied the correct pressure techniques." Under his disbelieving stare she wavered, sank back to the sand, and shut her eyes. "If you feel so grateful, leave me here and don't tell anyone you found me."

With a ragged sound of dismay at the mysteries hovering around them as persistently as gulls, he bent close to her and framed her face with his hands. One of his thumbs left a dab of his blood on her cheek; he shivered with the idea they had marked each other in some basic, unchangeable way.

Now shadowed by his body as he had been by hers, she half-opened her eyes and looked up at him, frowning. "I didn't mean to shoot you."

"I know."

She searched his expression for a moment. "I see. You don't want revenge. What do you want, really?"

"You. Everything about you, everything I see, and touch, and hear, everything I know and don't know—yet."

She blinked slowly, as if in a trance. "It would be easier if you admitted the truth. I have not had much honesty from the people who control my life. I would appreciate it from you, perhaps more than you can guess."

"*This* is honesty." He lowered his mouth to hers and kissed her gently, then feathered another kiss across her forehead. Whether she was hot from the sun or transmitting her special fire to him, he didn't know. She wasn't small or helpless looking, but right now she seemed frail, and one glance at her face told him he was upsetting her. "I'm your friend."

Audubon got to his feet, scrutinizing every detail of the bedraggled woman who had given his life back to him. His quick inventory of new information included her sinewy, strong feet and beautifully muscled calves. The floppy sack of a dress was slicked to curvaceous thighs and wadded between finely boned knees, revealing a tiny brown mole beside one knee-cap. It was an alluring beauty mark on her fair skin.

Looking closer, Audubon saw that her lower legs were sunburned and dirty from working in Beckel Nilly's field. Her bare arms were also that way.

She met his assessing gaze with eyes whose blue had faded from her odd spell of fatigue. Her mouth was drawn into a bitter line. "I can't run from you right now, and you know it."

"Yes. I don't understand it, but I'll have to wait until you trust me enough to explain. And this" —he pointed to the pink, star-burst scar on his side— "you have to explain it too."

"No. I'm through handing my pride over to others. What I can keep inside me, what few freedoms I have left, I will *keep*. You'll be very disappointed, and so will Kriloff, when you turn me over to him."

"You're not going back to him." Audubon became brusque, glanced up at the sky, and cursed the loss of time. "I'm sorry, but for now you'll have to believe whatever you like. We have to go."

The dinghy, dragging its small anchor, was just offshore. He brought it back and carried her to it. She slumped in the bow seat, hugging herself, as he cranked the motor. Farther out, the fishing boat floated peacefully. After Audubon hoisted her up the ladder, her knees collapsed and she sat down limply on the deck. He climbed into the boat after her and helped her rise to a cushioned seat along the side.

"I have some food in the refrigerator. Would eating make you stronger?"

"No. I'll be fine in a few minutes."

Fearing she might throw herself overboard when her strength returned, he quickly radioed the helicopter. The pilot had worked for Audubon for over a decade. He skillfully maneuvered the impressive machine, equipped with its pontoons for water landings, bringing it down no more than a dozen yards from the boat.

Turning her head wearily, Elena Petrovic pushed the hair from her face and moaned at the sight of the helicopter. "You *are* working for your government. How else could you have this?"

"I'm a disgusting capitalist with more money than you can imagine."

Audubon's pilot stared at his bloody trousers and the strange scar, but said nothing as he helped them board the helicopter. "What will become of your boat?" Elena asked Audubon as the pilot fastened a seat belt across her in the back passenger compartment.

"One of my people will take care of it later."

"One of your people? How many do you own?"

Audubon arched a brow. "One more than I owned before."

From the miserable expression on her face, he realized she had taken him seriously. She twisted away and stared out the window, placing one hand flat on the glass with the fingers spread in yearning. He stroked her shoulder soothingly, but she jerked away. "Have *one of your people* tell Mrs. Nilly some kind and apologetic lie about my departure, please."

"It will be taken care of. Don't worry."

"Everything will be taken care of for me." He saw a muscle work in the back of her jaw, as she ground her teeth. "How nice. I've heard that all my life. It's another way of telling me I have no choice."

Audubon watched her from the side as she fought and lost a battle to stop silent tears from slipping down her sunburned cheek. He wanted to touch her again, to take her in his arms and comfort her more than he'd ever comforted another human being, including himself. She'd nearly killed him, then saved his life, and whatever she'd done to accomplish the latter continued to renew him. Touching the scar on his bare side again, he had the disturbing idea that somehow she had put her spirit inside him . . . or had taken part of his.

What nonsense! He wanted to laugh but couldn't. The Russians were demanding she be found and returned, and he suspected that whatever made her valuable to them would make her doubly valuable to the State Department. If that was the case, Audubon needed her for some critical negotiations of his own.

No one at the State Department would hurt her. They'd be glad to help her defect. They'd simply expect her to cooperate in interrogation, to make herself useful. But that would be better than returning to Russia, wouldn't it? She'd be free, in a way. Tested, poked, prodded, spied on, and paraded in front of experts who'd find out all of her proud secrets, and then exploit them.

But she'd have more freedom, he told himself. And she'd understand, eventually, that she had helped him make a life-or-death deal, for a very good cause.

When the helicopter rose into the blue spring sky, she drew her fingertips along the window as if telling her hopes good-bye. Audubon lounged in the seat beside her, watching intently and beginning to dislike his merciless devotion to his work, no matter how noble. He struggled with a desire to protect her at all costs from anyone who might make her unhappy, including himself.

# *Three*

She had never flown in a helicopter before, and the noisy two-hour trip wore on her nerves. Her neck ached because she refused to turn away from the window and look at her captor. She spent the time picturing his "home," which she was certain must be some prison like laboratory or concrete government building filled with sinister servants who would spy on her.

And as she puzzled over his reasons for wanting her she hit upon the most logical answer: ransom. Elena knotted her hands in her dress. Of course! He said he was just a businessman, not a government agent. If that was true, then he must intend to *sell* her to Kriloff—or even to his own government.

She drew her conclusions and used them to build a wall. There would be no more demonstrations of her gift, and absolutely no more lowering of her guard with T. S. Audubon. He would get nothing from her until she decided how to use him for her escape. His seduction tactics wouldn't sway her.

Unless, by some impossible chance, they were sincere.

He put a hand on her shoulder. The careful, confident grip made her stomach drop—or was it the descent of the helicopter? Her expression frosty, she twisted to look at him. His pilot had given him a cotton undershirt to wear, but it was too small and accentuated the thick muscles of his shoulders and arms, making him look brawny and uncivilized. His hair, cut in long layers that reached the base of his neck in back, was disheveled and bore a streak of red from a careless stroke of his hand.

*A bloody barbarian,* she thought, but the image sparked her awareness of him as a man even more. His face, which she had never really had a chance to scrutinize closely before, had too many leathery creases and angles to be beautiful, but the mouth was cleanly sculpted, the nose noble, and the eyes large, with dark brown brows and lashes that curled up at the tips.

Those eyes, a warm green color, were watching her with soulful depth, yet as open and expectant as a puppy's. Mystified, she stared into them, searching for a way to trust him, wanting to trust him, and wishing suddenly that he and she didn't come from such different worlds. But this was no puppy, this was an elegant white wolfhound just waiting to taste her neck. *Proklyatnye!* And all his schemes could go to hell with him!

Elena pushed his hand off her shoulder. "Yes?"

"We'll be landing soon. We're flying over my estate. Look."

"Why should this make any difference to me?"

"It's not what you expected, I think."

Casually, but with a hidden undercurrent of intrigue, she craned her head and saw only forest broken with wide swaths of meadow. "Do you live in a tree?"

"I have so much land that you'd never tire of exploring it."

"If I was allowed to go where I wished."

"You will be."

The helicopter passed over a stone wall that ran through an alley in the forest as far as Elena could see. "Is your estate enclosed on all sides?"

"The central part, yes. I like my privacy."

"That wall looks rather high and unclimbable,"

she said with disgust. "A prison is a prison, no matter how much greenery you grow inside it."

"I'm not holding you prisoner, Elena, I'm *hiding* you."

"I was already hidden."

"Your people would have found you soon."

"The KGB are not 'my people.'" She thought of dear Sergei, who, though he'd been as affectionate as a grandparent with her, would do his duty regardless. "And what will happen if *your* people find me?"

"They won't. But eventually you'll have to ask the State Department for permission to stay in this country, you know."

"I will ask no one. They might send me back."

"No. They wouldn't do that."

"How do you know? You say you're not with the government. What gives you such assurance?"

"I'd have, hmmm, heard about it on *television* if we ever turned anyone down."

She thought there was a sly tone in his voice, but she couldn't be certain. The helicopter was too noisy to hear such subtle changes. "Such incidents are openly discussed?"

"Oh, yes. You should see our talk shows. Because of them, we keep up with everything from Russian defectors to the sex lives of men who wear skirts."

"You talk about *sex* on television?"

"Only between game shows, and usually before noon."

She frowned at the humorous glint in his eyes. "Well, I'm sure I'll see my story on television when you sell me to the highest bidder."

"Sell you? No." His expression turned serious, his eyes, shuttered. Elena's training at the institute had been designed to fine-tune her alertness to the emotional as well as physical energies that swirled within people. Now she easily read the truth in Audubon's expression.

He was going to use her in some way. There was no doubt. It troubled him, perhaps made him feel guilty, but he would do it. "Sell me, yes," she said wearily, but with sarcasm. "You terrible liar."

"I'm actually a magnificent liar, when the need arises. I'm afraid it's a talent my work requires. Not a dishonorable one, when used for the right purposes."

"Hah. You make importing and exporting things sound like a profession filled with intrigue."

"Yes." He leaned back in the heavily upholstered seat, stretched his long legs across her share of the small floor space, and linked his hands over his stomach. His invasion of her territory rattled her; his hooded eyes could hide his emotions much better than she'd expected. "I'm not going to sell you," he repeated.

"Then why are you interested in me?"

"You're beautiful, you're in danger, and you find me irresistible."

"Only one of those is correct."

"Then it will be very interesting to find out *which* one, won't it?" He smiled at her. "So, tell me why you expect me to sell you. You seem to think you're worth a lot of money. Is there a shortage of secretaries in Moscow? Do you type a thousand words a minute?"

"You think I'm worth a great deal. That's what I meant."

"I think you're worth much more than money. I *have* plenty of money."

"What don't you have, then?"

His smile became mysterious, teasing, sexual. "I'm still trying to decide."

The pilot glanced over his shoulder. "Home, sweet home."

Elena turned back to the window, her heart beating rapidly. An exclamation of surprise burst from her. They were only a short span above the treetops and closing in on an oasis of luxury in the middle of Audubon's wilderness. In front of them stretched beautiful lawns, gardens, ponds, white-fenced pastures dotted with horses, stables, and other outbuildings constructed in a style she'd seen in books about the English countryside.

And at the center of the estate rose a mansion built of stone and timber, its walls whitewashed so that the dark woods crisscrossed them in ornamental patterns with dramatic contrast. There were several stone chimneys, and a stone turret nestled into one of the mansion's nooks. It was a very welcoming and yet awe-inspiring place, surrounded by an apron of stone courtyard and patios. Everywhere were flower beds, manicured shrubs, and enormous trees.

She'd never seen anything as lovely and as . . . as *comforting*, she decided. How could anyone harm her in this country manor with its Edenlike setting? It seemed peaceful and safe. Except that Audubon would be with her. Or perhaps *because* he would be with her. Her head throbbed with confusion.

"You won't be unhappy here," Audubon said. "And you won't regret accepting my help."

Elena sank back on the seat, brooding about doubts—and temptations. "Whatever acceptance you get from me will cost you dearly." She raised proud eyes to his somber ones. "And money will be the least of it."

After he and she shared a tense, silent dinner— five courses, unfortunately—in the house's grand dining room, Audubon escorted her to her suite upstairs. They walked along a hall done in dark English antiques and colorful tapestries. There were no sounds, even their footfalls were silenced by the heavy carpet. "There are so many people in this house," she muttered. "How can it feel so empty?"

Her question disturbed him because he'd asked it himself in the past few years, but for a different reason. "There are only five people in the house full-time. And they're either at their jobs tonight or in their apartments in the downstairs wing. They don't come up here."

"But what do they all do? I understand the chef,

of course, and his assistant, and the housekeeper, but . . ."

"There's a security coordinator, and my personal secretary. You'll meet them tomorrow."

"Don't any of them have families? Wives? Husbands?"

"No. It's a condition of working for me. If they do marry, they can't bring their spouses here to live."

"But why?"

"It's my home, not an apartment building. And I can't have all sorts of strangers running around. This is my business headquarters."

"You lead a very odd life. You have no family, no wife—only people who work for you."

"My parents died some years ago. As for the wife part—I'm not a fan of marriage. And the nature of my business keeps me traveling a great deal. Marriage wouldn't work."

"What exactly do you import and export?"

He shrugged lightly. "Whatever pleases me." He wished he didn't have to lie to her. But even if she were an ordinary guest, he couldn't have told her the truth. There was simply too much at stake to allow information to spread beyond his highly trusted employees. The need for secrecy made for a lonely personal life, no matter how many women shared the perimeters of it, but Audubon had learned to accept loneliness as a child.

At the darkly paneled double doors to her suite, he stopped, looking down at her in the soft light from the frosted bulb in a silver wall sconce. Her unyielding pride had been knocked askew by the day's traumatic events; she returned his attention with sad eyes.

"This place does not suit me," she told him in her solemn, husky accent, like Greta Garbo playing *Ninotchka*. "I mean, I don't suit *it*."

"Where did you live in Moscow. An apartment?"

She looked away. "Oh, I . . . chose . . . to live at the institute. It's a grand old place, but nothing like this. I thought I had luxury because I had my own record player." She shook her head. "But then I came to America and saw everyone—even children—carrying those . . . those *boom* things . . ."

"Boom boxes? You mean the big cassette players?"

"Yes, those. Everyone has one. Amazing." She waved a hand at the furnishings around them, at his lifestyle. "And now this! You didn't make your fortune in some immoral way, did you?"

"Me, personally? No."

"What do you mean?"

"The Audubon family made its money the old-fashioned way—by exploiting other people. We started out in the fur trade, killing off the wildlife and cheating the Indians. Then we became planters and made a mint using slave labor. But we gave that up for the more honorable and profitable business of textile mills, employing young children."

"But you aren't repeating those shameful things. You've redeemed yourself by becoming a manipulative kidnapper. Take heart."

"Hmmm, sarcasm with a Russian accent. Don't tell me that you resent us capitalist pigs."

"No. I'm not political. Most Russians aren't, I suppose. I never got to know outsiders. I mean, people outside my own circle of friends."

"Hmmm. Now *there's* an interesting slip of the tongue."

She gave him a cool glance. "The only American I resent is *you*."

"Tomorrow I'll have some clothes and accessories brought in for you. And someone to fix your hair."

She was barefoot and wearing an oversized pink house dress that belonged to Clarice, his secretary. Clarice had also given her a pink barrette with which to pull the ragamuffin blond tresses back on one side. The amazing thing about Elena Petrovic was that she didn't seem more than mildly concerned about her parade of unflattering outfits.

And in fact, he was glad her clothes had hidden the charms underneath. It was troublesome enough to be fascinated with her mind and spirit without becoming obsessed with the rest of the package as well. But he was already losing that battle too.

"What are you going to do?" she asked bitterly. "Dress up the 'pigeon' to attract the hawks?"

"No, just make life easier on my sore eyes. Tell me—and don't be coy about having good taste—do you pick your own clothes?"

"No. I had no say in how I was dressed when you met me. And certainly none after I ran away."

He was startled. *I was a slave,* he recalled her saying. But he hadn't taken her words seriously.

"Good night," she said brusquely.

"Now, wait. You owe me an explanation for your last—"

"I owe you nothing. Nothing at all. I don't have to be nice to you. I don't have to care what you think of me."

It was true, and suddenly he realized she was unique in that respect. Everyone else either owed him something, wanted something from him, feared him, or respected him from a polite distance. She didn't give a damn about owing, wanting, fearing, or respecting, and so for the first time in years he could simply be himself, for better or worse. He loved it.

She nearly growled when he bent and kissed her quickly on the mouth. "Good night, fair damsel in disgusting dress."

She said something in Russian, and he was relatively certain it wasn't a thank-you. After she disappeared behind her suite doors, he stood outside in troubled thought, shocked by his rush of feelings of desire and loneliness.

He suspected she'd try to leave tonight, if for no other reason than to test the boundaries of her situation. She was nine parts courage and one part know-how, which he admired deeply, and he didn't want to humiliate her, so he'd let her get the adventure out of her system.

But when she tried her wings, he'd be there to stop her. It was really for her own good, he told himself. Really.

Did he think she was so smitten with him that she'd willingly stay? Elena was more angry than frightened when she tiptoed through the dark, imposing halls downstairs and easily unlocked the door to the outside.

Stepping onto a moonlit stone patio, she glanced around at the enormous swimming pool, cabana, and trellises covered with flowering vines. The grounds of the estate stretched beyond the back of the manor without a single obstacle to stop her. She had nothing to fear from the security lights around the stable and other outbuildings, and a Victorian streetlamp put out only a small pool of light in front of the cluster of guest houses nearby. The darkness was hers. She stared at the shadowy magnificence.

Whole houses just for guests! The man must have more money than sense. Why else would he recklessly allow her to wander?

Soon she was skirting the carpet of lawn at the edge of the forest, her bare feet wet with dew. She recoiled from the thought of walking for hours through the sharp, thorny, crunchy, invisible things that lay on the ground under the trees, but if Audubon thought having no shoes would keep her from leaving, he had sadly misjudged her determination.

Still, she was glad when she found a wide, man-made path. She decided to follow it through the woods at least until the moon rose a little higher. An hour later she was still hurrying along, and had to fight the eerie feeling she was lost in the middle of a deep green sea, being watched by sharks. No, not a sea, and not sharks. *Volks,* dangerous, majestic beasts with black fur—no, with white fur, and eyes as green as the forest, and dangerous intentions that the full moon encouraged.

The path rounded a curve and spilled into a meadow. The moon turned the opening into a silver bowl with dark sides made of forest. And in the center, waiting patiently astride a tall horse, was Audubon.

Elena stumbled to a halt, awed at the drama of the scene then consumed with rage. She'd never had a chance! He'd made a fool of her! She considered running, but already knew he'd catch her. Dignity wouldn't let her charge into the woods only to collide with trees and then be taken back to the house both bruised *and* defeated.

He nudged the horse and it walked toward her, switching its tail lazily, the English gear making the soft, taunting sighs of fine leather. "Good evening, Elena," Audubon said pleasantly. "Nice night for a walk, wouldn't you say? I had the same idea, myself."

The *volks* must spy for him, because no one else could have reported her route before she knew it herself. In bitter silence she turned and walked back to the path. His horse caught up with her without increasing its insultingly lazy gait. Its head bobbed along beside her, and the rhythmical whoosh of its breath was so patient that she wanted to scream.

"There's room for two up here." Audubon's deep, rich voice was also patient.

Twenty-five years of dreaming, hoping, and frustration, and defeat made her finally lose control. She stopped, threw her head back, and filled the night with a long wail of fury and grief. She saw a fallen limb to one side of the trail and snatched it up, then went to a tree and beat the branch against it with all her strength. She heard herself make keening sounds, and her head buzzed with desperation, closing out the rest of the world.

Then Audubon was behind her, enfolding her in his arms and pulling her against his torso while he gently grasped her wrists. She struggled against the restraint and the crooning sound he made into her ear, and doggedly held onto the limb, now splintered and bent.

"I won't be used any longer! I won't live without choices and dreams of my own, just my own, without having to ask for permission!"

"Tell me the truth," Audubon urged, holding her tightly, his mouth brushing her ear. "Were you part of Kriloff's research?"

"Yes! Yes! Are you satisfied, now? Does that confirm my value?"

"Did you volunteer to take part?"

She laughed with an edge of hysteria. "Volunteer? At five years old, would I *volunteer* to spend the rest of my life in captivity?"

"Elena, do you mean—"

"Stop! What difference does it make to you? You've always had everything you wanted. You've always lived in a country where people can do as they please!"

"Why are you so important to his work?" Audubon's hands slid over hers. She dropped the broken stick as his fingers pried into her palms. He cupped her hands inside his much bigger ones. "It's here, isn't it? What happened today on the beach came from something special inside you. *Tell me.*"

"Pay me." Her voice was cold. "Money, lots of it. And help me find a place to live. Then I'll tell you everything."

"I like *my* plan better. As soon as you get it through your head that I'm only going to help you, you'll talk. You can't go off alone and expect to be safe. My plan is for your own good."

"I'll never trust you, because you'll never admit your motive."

"You want a motive? Here." He took her by the shoulders, swung her to face him, then wrapped one arm around her shoulders and the other around her waist. With a suddenness that took her breath away she was on her tiptoes, her body conforming to his from chest to thigh. She could feel his leg muscles flex through her housedress and the tight riding trousers he wore. Winding her hands into his soft cotton shirt, she cursed years of training that magnified every nuance of his body to her senses.

"When we danced the other night, I wanted you in a pure male-wanting-female way," he whispered, his voice angry and challenging. "And you wanted me. I know you believe that, at least. Don't try to tell me otherwise."

"It's not enough."

"I don't have many purely personal pleasures in life, believe it or not, and I want to feel the way you make me feel. And that, my dear Elena, has nothing to do with your gift, or talent, or hocus-pocus—whatever you want to call the reason you're so valuable to Kriloff."

"You want sex, then? Okay, maybe I can trade sex for what I want." Crying silently, she caught his face between her hands and kissed him, hoping her limited experience wouldn't show. His mouth conveyed his surprise for a second, then his hands gripped her harder and he twisted his lips on hers, moving swiftly and taking the advantage in her small gasp.

There were dozens of emotions and sensations in the contact—the warm pull and push of his mouth, the defensive way she met his tongue with her own, then shivered with pleasure when his explored it tenderly. Fear shattered as the intimacy brought them so close, it seemed impossible to think of ever distrusting him again. Her knees were weak; she melted inward, aching. Elena rose farther on her toes, and the downward slide of his hand on her hips brought them closer. He nestled himself against her stomach, and she swayed. How could he give her this sublime combination of desire and emotion if he had other, less admirable, plans for her future? Surely he couldn't be that good at deception.

*Remember Pavel?*

It was easy to be blind when a man had you in his arms and you were dazed with instinctive responses to his touch. Such flights of fancy meant nothing, she knew. They were to be enjoyed, then forgotten. But Pavel had not been T. S. Audubon, and she'd never forget what Audubon's slow, uninhibited kisses were doing to her, even while she worried.

"You want to play games?" she asked. "Then we'll play." She reached between them with both hands and jerked the tail of his shirt loose, then quickly slid her hands underneath. This time, he was the one who drew a sharp breath. "I have power too," she warned. "A different kind." Molding her hands to his sides, she drew them upward. One found his half-healed scar; she poured her heat and energy into the place and heard him sigh in response.

"Part of your life belongs to me," Elena whispered, making it sound like a threat. "And I know you in a way that no other woman will ever know you." Her hands slid around him, the fingertips meeting over his spine. She tilted her head back and looked at him. The darkness hid his expression, but not the swift rise and fall of his chest. "I find an old back injury, here. The muscles stiffen sometimes."

She rubbed the pads of her fingers over the bone and sinew. "There, that's better." She brought her intimate hands down his back as if she'd stroked him a thousand times. Unerring, her right hand slipped under the waistband of his riding trousers. She never hesitated as her hand flattened just above his hip, her fingertips tantalizing the cluster of scar tissue there. "This nearly crippled you, and even though it didn't, I feel the arthritis that makes your leg ache sometimes."

"Your fingers are melting into my skin," he said hoarsely. "I can't tell where you stop and I begin. How do you do it?"

She pulled her hands away, raised them to his face, and stroked the backs of her fingers up his cheeks. "My secret. Don't think you have all the control."

"My God, no wonder Kriloff will do anything to get you back."

"And you will do anything to keep me—at least, until it suits you to do otherwise."

He grasped her hands and held them still, tucked against his chest. "I could turn you over to my own government. You could take your chances with the diplomats, hoping they won't give you back to Kriloff or let our scientists put you under a microscope. Or you can stay hidden here, as my guest. And I'll make sure that when my government does find out about you, you'll be given everything you want."

Poignant confusion tightened her throat. "I want to trust you, but you have too many mysteries."

"So do you." He stepped back, still holding her hands, and studied her in the moonlight. "But we have plenty of time to figure each other out."

"Do we, really? How long before someone learns I'm here?"

"I could hide you forever. I have the people, the know-how, and the money to take care of it. Don't worry."

"You've learned unusual skills from the import/ export business."

"No more unusual than your *massage* technique." He led her to the horse, climbed up while she stood in wary silence, then held out his hand. "You don't want to walk all the way home, do you?"

*Where will I ever have a home?* She wished he wouldn't be so casual with his sharing. When she left his estate, she didn't want to take homesickness for him and this place with her.

She exhaled in resignation and mounted the horse with his help, settling awkwardly behind him on the animal's wide back. "I'm no cossack. I can't ride. I don't even know what to hold on to."

"Me. That's the beauty of riding double. I get to have fun."

She grasped his bare sides where the shirt hadn't quite drifted back into place. This time she concentrated and kept her touch cool. But it was impossible not to savor the warmth and strength contained in the hard masculine body between her hands.

"You've turned the generator off," he noted slyly. "But the circuits are still humming."

During the ride back he tried to draw her into conversation, but she resisted until he finally gave up. She was more vulnerable to him than she'd suspected, and it frightened her. Years ago she'd stopped expecting the silver fox to come to her rescue; now she was too cynical to let herself imagine differently.

He escorted her to her suite a second time that night but didn't tease her with a kiss, as before. He didn't have to. He only had to stand there in the low, provocative hallway light and bid her good night, while his gaze lingered on her mouth. After she shut the door of the suite she leaned against it, listening to him walk away. His private quarters were on the other side of the house. He'd told her he kept the entire upper wing to himself. Lonely, mysterious Audubon. Did she dare believe he was a friend?

Dragging with fatigue and nervous exhaustion, she soaked her feet in a claw-footed bathtub in a bathroom larger than most Moscow apartments, with pale blue carpet as plush as the fur of a Russian sable. Tossing the housedress aside, she looked at herself in a gilt-edged mirror, seeing a raggedy blond woman in very plain, utilitarian white panties and a pointed bra.

American women didn't wear pointed bras. She hoped new underwear was part of the clothes Audubon had mentioned. It occurred to her that she was becoming very uncomfortable with the way she looked to him.

Frowning, she stripped off her underwear and sank into a canopied bed with sheets trimmed in white lace, and pillows almost as large as herself. The room's delicate white antiques stood out in the moonlight coming through an enormous bay window. The feel of the sheets and white satin coverlet made her naked skin flush with excitement.

Even after this terrible, exhausting day, which had left her trapped, alone, and fearing she'd revealed too much about herself, she felt a glimmer of hope. She thought of Audubon, analyzed him, mulled over his every word, every touch, the essence of him, and came to no conclusions. But she lay in the darkness, with the sheets making love to her skin, and watched a houseplant in one corner of the room begin to bloom.

# *Four*

His Majesty, also known as Mr. Rex, was inarguably the most renowned expert in beauty and fashion among the wealthy women of Virginia. His Richmond salon even drew the elite from Washington. On many occasions he'd been brought to Audubon's estate to tend a guest's coiffure. As far as Audubon was concerned, the only worthwhile reason to hire Mr. Rex was his fierce code of silence. He never talked about his clients to *anyone*, and neither did his well-trained staff.

"His Majesty's here," Clarice announced to Audubon when the housekeeper, Bernard, called downstairs with the news. "Bernie's cleared a place for him in the garden room because he insists on lots of natural light. Guess he'd get moldy in normal light. Ms. Petrovic has been brought to the throne room and is now being studied by His Majesty's court. Bernie says His Majesty shrieked when he saw her. I don't know if that's good or bad."

As Audubon stepped onto the main floor, eager to see Elena after spending a long morning in his underground office, he heard Rex shouting at an assistant. The perpetually exasperated voice echoed down the marble-tiled center hall from beyond the whitewashed arch that led to the glass-enclosed piazza across the back of the house.

"Use the *cream* facial, you twit! I said her skin was dry, not oily!"

Lost in his dark mood, Audubon couldn't manage even a disgusted smile as he strode toward the beauty battlefield. Winning Elena's trust and pampering her—if Mr. Rex's attention could be called pampering—would have been pure pleasure except for his ultimate goal.

He had *never* let personal feelings interfere with his decisions before, but now two separate dilemmas had become tangled into one large, distracting worry. There was Elena, a woman like no other, and the first in years who made him want to rediscover life beyond his work. And there was Kash Santelli, his adopted son, who might be in trouble on an assignment. Their futures depended on Audubon . . . and possibly on each other.

Audubon forced a smile as he entered the sprawling room filled with plants and white wicker furniture. In the center of a cleared circle, where antique wicker and lush greenery had been pushed aside as if to form an arena, Elena's tall, slender body was sunk into a special beautician's chair that Mr. Rex carted along on private appointments.

In Clarice's huge pink housedress she resembled an oversized bell with two slender clappers. Her bare legs stuck out from the knees down. They were propped on pillows atop the chair's padded footrest, and her toes, decorated with red polish on the nails, were separated by chunks of cotton. Her willowy arms lounged on pillows along the chair's armrests, and her fingers were also pried apart with cotton. Their nails bore no color—yet.

"I've seen cats do that with their claws." Audubon commented, halting nearby with his hands clasped behind him and his chin up. "You look as if you've just been startled by a puppy."

"A wolf," she said deadpan. "Good morning."

"Good morning." He was struggling not to chuckle. Then her line of vision, which had been blocked by Mr. Rex and a female assistant's fussy maneuvers around her head, swiveled toward him and locked. Audubon felt a surge of excitement through his nerves, his blood, his thoughts. She was studying him with less wariness and more hope this morning, and in the hope there was also the pure, elemental trading of unsatisfied questions, fears, and desires.

Troubling thoughts about the future tore at him. If he were forced to trade her to the State Department in return for favors in Kash's situation—and if she were as important as he suspected—the State Department would tuck her away someplace for safe keeping, with a new identity and government supervision. He might never see her again.

*Well, what if you married her? You could trade her, but get her back later.*

Marriage? He had let the *M* word cross his mind in reference to a woman he hardly knew, had just met a few days ago? He, the man whose feelings toward marriage were sarcastic, at best? Audubon rubbed his aching forehead and consoled himself with the knowledge that she'd never accept his proposal, anyway. A woman who talked of nothing but freedom wasn't likely to tie herself to the first American who offered.

"Do you have a headache?" she asked in her husky, quiet voice. There was a hint of challenge in it, but also sympathy. Mr. Rex's assistant was giving her a manicure, working now on her right hand. Elena lifted the left and waved the fingers at Audubon ever so slightly. *I could help your headache,* the gesture promised. Teased, a little. *I know where you hurt.*

Audubon smiled but shook his head. Her rich blond hair was set in tight marching regiments of permanent-wave curlers, and her face was an owlish mask of chalk-colored cream, leaving holes around her blue eyes and the tentative smile on her small, lush mouth. The warm light of the sun pouring through the glass ceiling bathed both of them in its intimate glow, as if they were alone in the room, in the world.

But they weren't. A slew of people and problems stood between them. He took a deep breath and looked away, trying to regain his composure. It was even more unsettling to be hypnotized by a woman who, at the moment, resembled a member of some primitive tribe who'd decorated herself for a chastity dance. "Are you comfortable?" he asked.

"I am being tortured," she replied dryly.

Audubon stepped closer, nodding hello to Mr. Rex, whose pompadour of auburn hair, beaked nose, and bright Hawaiian shirt made him resemble a colorful, flapping parrot. "She's *such* a dream under all that ragged hair," Mr. Rex gushed. "I cut about four inches off of it. I can't *wait* to see her unrolled and fluffed."

"This is safe, this unrolling and fluffing?" she asked solemnly.

Audubon sighed. "Only if you cooperate."

Mr. Rex flung his hands up in delight. "Oh, and just *wait* until we get rid of those tacky clothes and start trying on some of the gorgeous things on the racks my people are setting up in the main living room. My darling ladies are going to have such fun dressing you. They'll treat you like a Barbie!"

She had never taken her eyes from Audubon, even as she listened to the ever-talking Mr. Rex. Her gaze continued to draw Audubon's concentration, even surrounded by ten tons of white goo. Now he watched her eyes narrow in thought. "What is a Barbie, and how do Americans treat it?"

"It's a classic and beloved doll for children," Audubon assured her.

"I hope you're not shy about being stared at in your lacies," Mr. Rex interjected, squirting a foul-smelling solution on her curlers.

"What are lacies? Clothing that has laces in it?"

"Lingerie," Audubon explained, and found himself imagining her in 'lacies' with a vividness that made the unflattering pink housedress disappear. "But we can certainly get you some kind of lingerie that laces up, if you're interested. You might need help getting out of it every night, though."

"Oh, my," Mr. Rex said, chortling.

She looked away, undone by Audubon's counter-attack, and laughed. "I'll have to learn your slang very quickly, so I won't get into trouble."

"Well, we have lots of *respectable* underthings for you to try on," Mr. Rex continued. "And the ladies won't make you feel like a striptease artist while they help you choose, I promise."

"I'm used to being examined—I mean, I'm not shy about having people look at me," she said. Audubon saw the cosmetic mask pucker between her eyes as she frowned. She stared at the cobblestone floor as if lost in memories, unpleasant ones. His stomach twisted with a quiet, deep need to comfort her, though she hadn't asked for comfort.

"Well, you're certainly a good sport about sitting here like *this*," Mr. Rex said cheerfully, as he covered the curlers with a plastic cap. "Most women would be screaming if dear Mr. Audubon had ventured into this room."

She shot Audubon a troubled glance, then set her gaze on a white, wrought iron baker's rack filled with African violets. "I'm sure that Mr. Audubon likes to startle his women."

There was enough humor in her voice to show she wasn't too bothered by his scrutiny. She *ought* not to affect him, dammit! And she didn't seem to care whether she had to parade naked in front of a small army of female strangers who would tamper with her from head to toe in pursuit of fashion perfection.

Audubon loved her sensible lack of discomfort at the same time that it worried him. For some reason he was reminded of Kyle Surprise, a former agent who'd been hurt badly during an assignment. Audubon had visited him during each of his hospital stays for plastic surgery. Kyle had grown so resigned to having his entire body exposed to the scrutiny of medical personnel that by the last hospital stay he had sat in bed naked, chatting unconcernedly with

Audubon, while a doctor and several interns studied his scars. It was as if he'd learned to check his dignity at the admissions desk.

Kyle was doing fine now, despite the scars that even surgery couldn't conquer. His strength of character and the love of his new wife and daughter had pulled him through. Audubon frowned, wondering why Elena's reaction to this undignified but hardly unpleasant situation would make him think of Kyle's stoicism.

"Mr. Rex, give me a minute alone with your noble victim, please. She and I have something to discuss. It can't wait."

Mr. Rex sighed. "Only a minute. I wouldn't want her perm to fry."

"Fry?" Elena repeated, her voice rising.

"You'll be fine," Audubon told her. After Mr. Rex and his assistant left, Audubon pulled a wicker chair close to hers. He sat down while she straightened in guarded reaction. Leaning toward her, he put a hand on her arm and squeezed gently as he held her shuttered gaze. "You said you were one of Kriloff's research subjects."

She nodded, and her proud shoulders never flinched. "One of many, yes."

"Since you were five years old?"

"Yes."

"And you lived at the institute—you had no choice?"

"That's right. He tries to make his people believe they're partners in his work, but in effect, they are only prisoners. I was never allowed to leave the institute without supervision."

"What about school, a social life? . . ."

"Tutors were brought in. I had classes with several other children like me. They were also my playmates."

"Like you? Paranormals?"

"Yes."

"What happened to your parents?"

Her fingers curled and uncurled in between the cotton packing. Despite her ridiculous appearance, she radiated dignity that took his breath away. But she seemed to be reconsidering her openness. "Why are you asking me these questions now?"

"I want to know what happened to make you so casual about your body."

"Casual?"

"You act as if you're accustomed to having people touch you, look at you, do things to you that others might find very embarrassing."

She shifted in the chair, looked at him hard for a second, then shut her eyes. "I am accustomed to it all."

He winced. He wasn't certain he wanted to know more, but he was driven to understand her. "I've read about the doctor's theories. He says that paranormal powers are simply an exaggerated form of the electromagnetic energy all of us produce."

"Yes." She opened her eyes swiftly. "We all share such powers. Some people, like me, have more than normal energy, and can focus it. But I'm impressed you know that."

"And so he studies the physical and mental aspects as well as the psychic."

"Yes."

"Which means . . ." He stopped, an ugly taste in his throat. Her arm was icy under his hand.

"Which means," she continued for him, speaking slowly and with emphasis, "that I've undergone every medical test imaginable, been studied inside and out routinely all my life, and learned to give up the privacy of my body as well as my mind. Yes, I'm accustomed to being naked in front of groups of impersonal strangers, and yes, I learned *many* years ago to accept whatever was done to me in the name of science. I had no choice."

She ducked her head and stared at her lap. He was glad she wasn't looking at him any longer. He had tears in his eyes. "You'll never be treated that way again," he said hoarsely. "I swear it." Her gaze rose to his face as he continued headlong into his reckless promise. "I'll die before I let you go back to that kind of life."

A small shocked and anguished sound of amazement burst from her lips. "Audubon," she whispered. "Audubon."

Mr. Rex emerged from a doorway to another garden room. He called, "I really *am* sorry to intrude, but I have to check a test curl. I don't want her to frizz."

"I wouldn't want to frizz," she murmured, tears sliding into the white goo as she continued to gaze at Audubon.

"Absolutely not." He cleared his throat roughly and stood up. Suddenly her arm warmed beneath his hand. "So you have excess electromagnetic energy," he said, his voice gruff and distracted. "That hardly explains how miracles happen."

"Kriloff believes miracles can be pinned to a display board, like strange insects, then dissected."

"He's a fool." Audubon drew his fingertips off her skin, and the heat seemed to follow him. His head swam; it was all he could do to stop himself from chasing everyone out of the house and locking him and her in together, alone, so that they could talk and touch and share all the mysteries of their lives.

"We'll talk more, later," he told her, stepping back shakily. "Would you like to have dinner with me tonight?"

She ordered up a small, trembling smile. "Yes. It will be interesting to see what you think of me after all of this . . . this *fixing* is done."

"I think you're magnificent already." He left the garden room on rubbery legs.


The phone console buzzed. Clarice turned toward her rosewood desk and answered the phone. Her side of the conversation intrigued Audubon so much that he found himself leaning forward on the edge of his chair. She tossed the receiver back onto its rest and hooted with disgust. "Mr. Rex has been sniffing a bit too much hair spray, I'd say."

"What happened?"

"Nothing. He admits he was the only one who saw it. Elena was staring after you at the time."

Audubon grasped the edge of his desk. "What did he see?"

Clarice slapped her silk skirt and laughed. "He said one of the African violets 'exploded' into bloom."

She was a different person now, and not just because she'd finally escaped from Kriloff. Everything she knew about herself, about her responses as a woman, about her fears and goals for every part of her life, was confused because of Audubon.

Freedom was still her guiding light; she'd never jeopardize the chance to have it—to go where she wished, have a job, make her own living, make her own decisions. But wasn't it possible she could have Audubon, along with the rest? Did he think of her as someone he wanted to know better—not as a project, but as a friend and lover?

Elena looked at the transformed person in the floor-to-ceiling mirror in her suite's bath and wasn't certain what she was becoming. Whatever it was, it felt strong and optimistic. But it felt dangerous also. Freedom—or at the least the prospect of it—was a heady thing.

Downstairs, the evening sun glinted through the beveled glass of the open French doors. The stalwart Bernard, dressed in his housekeeper's uniform of patent shoes, black slacks, and a crisp white shirt with a gold tie, ushered her onto a patio by one of the pools, set in natural stone with a man-made waterfall at one end. Tall lamps with Victorian fixtures were beginning to flicker into life. She realized they were some modern wonder that responded to the setting sun.

She felt the same way, her excitement growing

brighter as she waited for Audubon to reach her personal horizon.

Bernard stood patiently beside her, watching her wide-eyed appraisal of the place. He had a small team of maids and valets who scurried around during the day, doing the menial chores; he seemed to be a general, and she tried not to stare at him in awe too. He was graying and dignified and very much like a picture she'd seen of Sir Laurence Olivier.

"You look absolutely lovely, Miss Petrovic," he said sincerely, guiding her toward a table set with linen, crystal, and a spray of white orchids in a short, porcelain vase.

"Thank you. I am overwhelmed by the change myself." The patio was surrounded by beds of tulips; draping willow trees whispered as their green tresses swayed in a hint of breeze. The sunset's golden light bronzed the pool's surface. Elena's senses were already drunk with stimulation, and Audubon hadn't even arrived yet.

She touched Bernard's arm as he pulled a chair from the table and nodded toward it politely. "Please, I'm too nervous to sit down right now. May I ask you some questions about Mr. Audubon?"

"Certainly." He smiled, but she read the polite restraint in his expression. This man, like everyone else who worked for Audubon, belonged to his loyal inner circle of trusted allies. They wouldn't reveal anything Audubon didn't want revealed.

"Have you worked for Mr. Audubon a long time?"

"Ah! Since the Sphinx was a pebble! I came to work at Grace Hall when Mr. Audubon's father was a young man, years before Mr. Audubon was born."

"Grace Hall?"

"The original Audubon estate. A magnificent Southern mansion. It dated from seventeen eighty-two. It's located not far from here."

"Who lives there?"

"Mr. Audubon sold it to an international investment group twenty years ago. It's become a country club."

"But . . . it had such tradition, such sentiment. Why did he sell it?"

Bernard's cordial expression stiffened a little. "I'm sure Mr. Audubon would prefer to answer these questions himself. It's a . . . tragic story."

"His parents are dead?"

"Yes, for many years."

"They had no other children?"

"There was a younger child, a sister to Mr. Audubon, but she died in a ski lift accident in Switzerland when Mr. Audubon was only twelve."

"How sad."

"Yes." The increasing reluctance in Bernard's face told her there might be another unpleasant story behind the sister's death. "Well," he said brusquely, smiling, "I shall go and make certain that Mr. Audubon knows you're waiting . . ."

"Was it a happy family?"

Bernard studied her in silence, as if assessing her right to know. Then he said softly, "No, it was always a most *un*-happy family, Miss Petrovic. Why do you ask?"

"I want to understand him."

"He's a very fine man despite his family, but also *because* of it. Sometimes the saddest upbringing molds the strongest character."

"I like to think so, myself."

"Your parents? . . ." Bernard let his words hang, a question.

She shook her head. "My father was killed in a factory accident when I was a baby. My mother was a schoolteacher, but she disappeared when I was five. I hardly remember her. But what I remember is very good."

"She *disappeared*?" Audubon asked.

Elena pivoted, startled to see Audubon between the open French doors. "Please, don't spy on us," she teased after a second. Her heart beat wildly. His slow, inscrutable examination of her new look could be disapproval or disappointment. It was very intense. "I have so few secrets left," she added.

"I'm sure that's not true."

He crossed the patio to her and Bernard, who stepped back, smiled, and glided into the house. She smoothed sweaty palms over her trim, black skirt. It was knee-length and rather demure, she thought, except that she'd never worn a skirt made of leather before. She hoped that he didn't think her too prim in the plum-colored blouse with its billowing sleeves and buttoned collar. Suddenly she wished that she'd worn high heels instead of black flats. And lighter-colored clothes. American women dressed so cheerfully for spring, but she, like an ignorant peasant, had chosen purple and black!

He was dressed in a handsome casual shirt with large, graceful pockets on the chest and rolled up shirt sleeves. It heightened the width of his chest at the same time that the drape of it scooped dramatically into his well-honed waist, surrounded by the slender belt he wore with pleated tan trousers.

His studied casualness whispered of strolls past cafés on the Riviera, of comfortable elegance lounging in the seat of a Ferrari, of sheer masculine confidence combined with very old, very aristocratic money. She began to get a headache.

"You look very ethnic," he said, stopping in front of her. "The blouse is very . . . cossack. Yes. You're a very attractive female cossack, even if you don't know how to ride a horse." He paused, and now that he was little more than a pace away, she saw the admiration that made his green eyes glisten like polished jade. "And your hair . . ."

He lifted a hand and ran his forefinger along the wavy strands that ended in a gently blunt style at her jawline. Mr. Rex had told her to keep the side part, but he'd performed some kind of cutting magic so that her thick hair only draped to the outside edge of her brow. She no longer had to peer through it or yank it back with barrettes.

She almost wished for its privacy screen. Audubon's admiration and the closeness of his body made her quiver inside; the look in his eyes sent direct signals to every reckless impulse she'd never been able to indulge before—and had never wanted so badly to indulge now.

But she kept her eyes trained on his, scolding him for trying so openly to hypnotize her, scolding herself for being such a gullible kitten, eager for stroking. "I was investigating you," she warned. "If you hadn't shown up so soon, I would have pried all of your secrets out of poor, unsuspecting Bernard. I am actually a Soviet spy, you know, and very tricky. My code name is Red Delilah."

"Oh? I thought the Kremlin would have named you the Anti-Stealth Pigeon." He chuckled so warmly that she bit her lip but smiled regardless. "Turn that lip loose," he commanded, his expression mischievous. "Or I might have to rescue it."

She moved away a little, not wishing to push her recklessness too far, and dabbed at her new lipstick with hot fingertips. "You're a great deal of fun, but all American men are that way, I've heard. Playboys."

"And all Russian women are either sly, cold vipers or dumb cows. They get messy-drunk on vodka and dig potatoes for fun. And they grunt when the walk."

"What a lie!"

"Of course it is. Turnabout is fair play. That's an old American saying. Memorize it." Behind his rebuke he was laughing at her, at them both, and she began to laugh too.

"I can only judge you by what I've been told about American men, Audubon. I'm sure I have many mistaken ideas, but you'll have to prove them wrong one at a time."

"But you see, I don't have any mistaken ideas about *you*. So one of us, at least, can move ahead without worrying. Now, about your mother—what do you mean, 'She disappeared'?"

Elena looked at him wistfully. "She was in trouble with the police. She wasn't Russian, she was Lithuanian, and they said she belonged to an underground group that promoted the old way—separatism, independence."

"Everything that's happened in Lithuania during the past years shows she wasn't the only rebel."

"But she was a rebel twenty-five years ago, when people kept quiet about their beliefs. Imagine, she'd lived in Moscow most of her life, but they accused her of being a traitor."

"She ran from the police?"

"That's what they said. They came to school one day and took me out of class. They took me to our apartment and showed me that all her clothes were gone. A few days later they sent me to Kriloff's institute, just outside the city."

"But how did they know about your . . . I don't know what to call it. What do you call it?"

"Sometimes I call it a curse, but usually I think of it as a gift. All I remember is that I came down with a fever when I was five, and I almost died. Afterward, I wasn't . . . I wasn't the same. I could do things I hadn't done before, things no one else could do. Mother took me to a pediatrician and asked for help, but he laughed at us. A few weeks later, Mother left."

"And you were taken straight to Kriloff's institute?" Audubon put a hand on her shoulder and asked softly, "Do you think what the police told you was true?"

Elena shook her head. "I've wondered ever since. I'll never know for sure. It's hard, not knowing." The loss of her mother, and her fear that it was connected to her gift somehow, was an old, grinding pain inside her chest. She hugged herself. With all the jeopardy in her current situation, she couldn't brood about the past as well. "But about *your* parents . . ."

"Oh, no. It's time for the pre-dinner floor show." He pulled her chair out and gestured gracefully.

"You are a manipulative man who values his privacy much more than you value the privacy of others."

"I have an unusual number of dastardly deeds to hide. Silence, Anti-Stealth Pigeon."

Shaking her head, she sat down, never taking her eyes from him, one brow arched in dismay. "What are you going to do?"

"Demonstrate my musical talent. Some call it a curse; I call it a gift." He retrieved a violin and bow from the seat of the opposite chair. Tucking the violin under his chin, he peered down at her with a quaint expression. "I'll be your strolling musician. Only I'll stand still." He clicked the heels of his burnished loafers. "Miss Petrovic, Mozart and I welcome you to America."

He began to play, and she was surprised at how good he was. Excellent, really. The piece was slow and lyrical. Watching his large, brutally built fingers coax the delicate instrument made streamers of sensation wind around her. Before long she was leaning forward, her lips parted, her body longing to dance a pas de deux with him.

Ballet had been her pastime, her savior from the long, lonely hours of winter, when she was so rarely allowed to leave the institute, and her imitation of freedom. When she practiced at the bar in the small studio Kriloff had created for her, she felt that no force could contain her.

Now, lost in Audubon's music and charisma, she knew that he could lead her to real freedom—or if she were wrong about him, to desperate disappointment. When he finished and lowered the violin to his side, she stood shakily. They were silent, looking at each other in breathless anticipation.

"This pigeon will try to trust you," she whispered.

His eyes glowed. "Not a pigeon. A dove. Thank you for trusting me. You won't regret it."

She stepped close to him, raised on tiptoe, and kissed his cheek. He made no move to pull her to him, but the slow caress of his eyes did it for him. Elena savored his mouth with a lengthy kiss, slicking her tongue between his welcoming lips, exploring him with a finesse borne of both tenderness and greed. She put her hands on his waist and slid them upward, until her sensitive fingers found the scar under his right rib cage.

He sighed into her mouth as she pressed her hot, healing hand over the scar, communicating with him in that vulnerable way while she continued to kiss him. *Be everything I need for you to be*, she begged silently. *Be as wonderful as you seem.*

"Mr. Audubon, excuse me. It's urgent," Bernard said from the doorway.

Elena drew back, sorry that the intimacy had been witnessed, even by Bernard. So few things in her life had been private. Feeling Audubon's breath on her temple, she raised her eyes to his and found a similar regret. *"Nyezabvyonniy,"* he said, distorting the word absurdly with his Rhett Butler drawl.

Delight rushed into her throat. "Unforgettable. I agree."

"Mr. Audubon, Clarice says you have a call from Mexico," Bernard interjected in a diplomatic but hurried tone.

Audubon's mood changed in an instant. He tossed the violin and its bow into a chair. "I'll be back," he told Elena, but strode into the house without another glance at her.

"I'll bring you some canapés and a glass of wine, Miss Petrovic," Bernard offered, sounding as if she might have a long wait.

Bewildered, she walked to the edge of the pool and gazed blankly at the waterfall. Audubon's mysteries filled her with dread. She trusted him, yes. *Yes.* She had to trust someone in this country, after all, and what ulterior motives could he possibly have? He didn't need more money, power, or business success.

She searched for more reassurance, more logic, until finally she admitted that there was nothing logical about her trust in him. She was falling in love as if the first twenty-nine years of her life had been building up to it all along, and what she'd felt for Pavel seemed like a poor joke. This time she'd lose much more than a few layers of pride if she was wrong.

He took the stairs rather than the elevator down to the complex of offices beneath the main floor, then paced the intricate patterns of the Persian rug in his office.

In her whiskey-and-peanuts voice Clarice ordered, "Put your rump on the powwow blanket, Chief, and stop shakin' your feathers."

He threw a grim smile at her. She sat at her computer with her silk skirt hiked above her knees, her imported pumps tossed in the corner under a bank of televisions tuned to various national and international news shows, with the sound turned down. She frowned at the computer screen and chewed the tip of a gold pen that she usually kept tucked in her gray chignon. She was the widow of a Texas police captain, a former data-processing specialist for the CIA, and a crack poker player.

Now, as a light blinked rapidly on the computer's telephone modem, she squinted at the screen and muttered a word that would have scared rattlesnakes off a warm rock. "They're saying that Kash was seen Friday at the de Valdivia hacienda not far from Tuan. If that's where he is, he's in more trouble than we thought."

Audubon stopped pacing to pound a fist against the side of a lacquered bookcase filled with reference volumes. In an open space between them were personal photographs of friends, celebrities, politicians, and the photo of an exotic, fiercely handsome young man with a braid of black hair hanging over the shoulder of his Armani suit. Kash Santelli, twenty-six, wasn't quite young enough for Audubon to think of him as a son, but since he and Douglas Kincaid had smuggled the outcast Vietnamese-Egyptian-American boy out of Vietnam nearly twenty years ago, he was family to both of them.

Last year Kash had grown restless working in Douglas's rather conservative business empire; despite a master's degree in business from Harvard he felt that he had much more to prove to a world that had often mistreated him. When Kash had asked to work for him, Audubon had agreed reluctantly. He tried to maintain an emotional distance between himself and his people, though he was deeply protective of them; with Kash, the barrier was impossible to maintain, and he constantly worried about the young man's safety.

"If Traynor doesn't locate him by this afternoon, I'm going to Mexico."

Clarice snorted. "I'll call every one of the team who isn't up to his or her eyebrows in business and have them here before you set one toe out the front gate. They'll hold you down. It'll be a war party of your own braves, Chief. You'd be in more trouble than Kash, if you went! You *know* that. Let our folks handle it. They're the best. You trained them all, remember? And *you're* the best."

"Except for this time, you mean. I'm not objective."

"Well, yes. But I understand why. You've never had to worry about a member of your family before."

"My *only* family."

He slumped into a richly upholstered swivel chair and raked both hands through his luxurious hair, leaving it completely disheveled, which his vanity would ordinarily have never allowed. All he could think about was Kash versus Elena, and he prayed that he wouldn't have to use her to save his adopted son.

"I'm going to Mexico tonight," he called to Clarice.

By the time Audubon returned, Elena had finished her wine and nervously eaten half a plate of toastpoints piled with smoked salmon while she paced by the pool. She was accustomed to hearty, slow, sit-down meals, not "grazing," as the Americans like to call their fondness for nibbling on the run, but she wanted to learn to eat as Americans did.

She halted, staring at Audubon's approach. Already uncomfortable and worried, she grew even more upset as he took her hands and raised them to his lips for a cool, distracted kiss. His face was drawn because of some private problem; he had aged and become harsh looking in just an hour's time. His tall, athletic body was wound tight; every movement conveyed command and swift action. "I have to leave on a business trip to Mexico. I apologize."

"Business? This evening? Your import/export company demands such emergency action?"

"Yes."

"Will you return soon?"

"I don't know." He swept a frowning gaze over her alarmed and wary reaction. "A little while ago you said that you trusted me. I assumed that you meant it."

"I trusted a different man from the one who took a mysterious phone call. How can you expect me to feel secure among secrets? Does this trip have anything to do with me?"

"No."

"If Kriloff discovers I'm here while you're gone, what will happen?"

"Nothing. Elena, I don't have time to be diplomatic. Here are the bare facts—very little that you do outside your own suite goes unwatched. I have people working here whom you never see, but they see you. They'll make certain no one comes here to take you away."

She drew her hands from his. "And they'll also make sure I don't escape. While the master is gone, the servants will spy."

"All right, look at it that way, if you want. Hell, you don't even know where you'd go if you *did* get your precious freedom. And I assure you, before you had time to enjoy it, you'd be caught, reprimanded, and shipped back to Russia at Kriloff's request. I think I have a little better future to offer you than he does."

"I'll make my own future."

"For the time being, you'll do as I say." He grimaced at those words and reached for her hands again. She snapped them out of range, cursed him in Russian, and stepped backward proudly.

Right into the pool.

He dropped to his heels as she splashed to the

surface, slinging her newly cut hair out of her eyes. The water was only chest-deep. She righted herself and shot him a burning look of humiliation and fury. "Go!"

"I'm sorry. I wish you found something funny about this," he said. But there wasn't a trace of humor in him either. "I'll tell Bernard to bring you a towel. I don't have the time or patience."

He rose, pivoted, and went back into the house, while she stared after him in complete shock, realizing that she didn't know him at all.

# *Five*

Elena was wary when Audubon sent an apology the next day, particularly because the apology was delivered by a woman.

Elgiva Kincaid, the wife of Audubon's friend Douglas, arrived with considerably less fanfare than Elena expected of a billionaire businesswoman. Elgiva toted her own suitcase through the double doors of the front entrance, despite Bernard's protest. Her long auburn hair spilled from under a broad sun hat that matched her white T-shirt and overalls. An enormous diamond wedding ring she wore on her left hand lent interesting contrast to the overalls.

"Very American, wouldna' you say, lass?" she noted, pointing to herself as Elena stared. Her Scottish burr sang with good cheer. "Audubon asked me to come and have a visit with you while he and my Douglas are off on business together. I suppose he thinks a fellow female can talk you into relaxing. Men! They do no' understand us, sometimes, do you think?"

"I don't understand *him*, either."

"There's a wise lass. We'll be friends."

As they drank mint tea in the manor's white-on-white breakfast nook, Elena tried to compose tactful questions about Audubon and Douglas Kincaid. "Are they doing something illegal?"

Elgiva Kincaid almost bit the edge of the china cup. "My husband's no criminal, lass, and neither is Audubon. Agh! If you're asking me to explain Audubon to you, you've come to naught. In most ways he's as much a mystery to me as when I met him, and that was two years ago." Elgiva chuckled. "You see, Audubon doesna' approve of marriage, and the poor, misguided man is keeping to himself now that most of his cronies have found wedded bliss."

"It's something to do with his parents, isn't it? There was something wrong with their marriage?"

Elgiva's ruddy, beautiful face saddened. "Let Audubon tell you about that, lass. 'Tis a dark tale, and I only know it because Douglas told me. Audubon never discusses it, just as he never tells what the 'T. S.' stands for. Not even Douglas knows, and they've been friends since Vietnam."

"Can't *anyone* tell me about Audubon?"

"I would, lass, I swear it, but I owe him too much."

Elena's hands rose to her throat. "Money?"

"You think dear Audubon is a blackmailer? No, I mean he helped bring Douglas and me together. It was a messy situation between us, and Audubon pushed us in the right direction. Despite his grumbling about marriage, he can no' resist promoting true love, as long as it's not for himself."

"Can you tell me that story, at least?"

"Oh, a wee bit here and there. And I'll tell anything else Audubon wouldna' mind. Hmmm. For instance, Audubon and my own wonderful Douglas were heroes in the Vietnam War. Audubon was a grand leader, Douglas says. He used to recite epic poetry—when the fighting wasn't on, of course—and the men called him 'Ashley Wilkes' behind his back." Elgiva looked at her dubiously. "Do you know 'Ashley Wilkes,' from the famous American book about the Civil War?"

"Oh, yes! But I call him Rhett Butler!"

"Well, I dunna' pretend to understand Audubon, either way. But Douglas said the men would follow him to hell, if he asked."

"He must have asked. He was wounded just above his left hip."

"Yes, leading an attack. And my Douglas carried him to safety. How did you know?"

"I only know about the scar. It's terrible."

The announcement that she had learned the rather intimate location of Audubon's old wound made Elgiva Kincaid lift both eyebrows and try to diguise her curious expression. "Lass, you being here, in his sanctuary, where few strangers have ever been allowed, and the intensity in his voice when he talks about protecting you . . . well, it adds up to a unique situation."

Elena gave her a beseeching look. "When he comes back, I have to be ready."

"Ready for what?"

Elena stared grimly out of a picture window at his fantasy world. The stable manager was exercising one of Audubon's thoroughbreds. The gardener was at work on an enormous plot of flowering shrubs. But beyond the grounds, the forest closed in, hiding the unbreachable stone wall deep within. "I'm not sure," Elena replied finally. "That's the problem."


It was two A.M. The manor was filled with lonely silence, and Elgiva had long since gone to her suite in the other wing. Worrying about Audubon, Elena stood at the deserted end of the hallway outside her suite, one hand balanced on a ponderous teak table in front of a picture window, the other hand extended in front of her as her bare, pointed foot drew ballet figures on the tapestry rug.

She liked the peaceful, shadowy hall and the knowledge she could go anywhere in the house she wished. Small freedoms. Her white silk nightgown was a mischievous influence, causing her to tuck her chin and watch as it clung to the length of her slowly moving leg. Always, her thoughts returned to Audubon. If she could only trace his patterns as easily!

"So you *do* know how to dance," Audubon said from the far end of the hall. His deep voice, though soft, reverberated off the paneled walls. She brought her feet together with a hurried snap and whirled to face him, instinctively pressing herself against the table behind her as if to make a fighting stance. Her hands braced on the edge, she drew a long breath as he walked toward her with his easy, confident stride, his hands hanging calmly by his sides.

"How long has it been?" he asked, shaking his head. "Three days since I left? I feel as if I haven't seen you in years."

His gaze took in all of the simple sheath night-gown, from the thin straps barely caught on her shoulders to the loosely draped bodice and flowing skirt. She had too much pride to huddle as if ashamed he'd caught her dressed this way and performing ballet exercises in the hall.

"Beautiful," he said, coming to a halt, a stride away. "The dance, the dancer, the gown. All beautiful."

With a hidden sigh of resignation she admitted that every fiber in her body was humming. The combination of sexual innuendo and polite restraint in his admiration was irresistible. She silently admitted she was glad the gown revealed a detailed outline of all it covered.

"I didn't have the proper clothes for practicing. Ballet is my hobby."

"From a male perspective I say you have the *perfect* clothes for practicing."

She heard his lighthearted tone, but as she studied his face she knew it was a facade. His skin was gray with exhaustion; glancing down, she saw that his clothes, an oddly Latin combination of white trousers and a white shirt with tiny, colorful, glass buttons, were wrinkled and streaked with dust.

"I should have changed before I came up here," he said, his voice raw, probably from too much talking and too little sleep. "But I was hoping you'd still be awake. I want to apologize for the other day."

The gown was his ally. It stroked her skin with his

sincerity. Oh, how she wanted to believe in him! Elena shook her head in a gesture that dismissed the incident at the pool. "I'm doomed to be in some awful state of 'dis-dress' every time we're together. It's only appropriate my new outfit and I should have been a flop."

"Not a flop. A splash." Chuckling hoarsely, he amazed her by suddenly sitting down on the floor. He did it in a single, limber movement that nonetheless couldn't conceal the slump of fatigue in his body.

"Audubon?" she asked anxiously. Elena had never expected to see him like this. Her swift fear for his condition made her drop to the floor near him, hugging her knees to her chest. "Did you just return from your Mexican trip? I mean, just a few minutes ago?"

He nodded. "Walked in, came straight up here." He smiled, but it didn't reach his eyes. "I thought you might loan me a cup of excess optimism. I'll gladly repay you on Tuesday for a tingle today . . . oh, never mind. You've never seen a Popeye cartoon."

Leaning against the polished wood as if it were the most luxurious pillow in the world, he gracefully jackknifed one long leg and then the other, pulling off his dusty white boots. Even his white socks were red with dirt. He tossed the boots aside, stretched his legs out and crossed them at the ankles.

Finally, his eyes half-shut, he looked at her again. "How are you? Do you like Elgiva? I hope she reassured you about your safety here."

"I am . . . open-minded. Let's leave it at that." She leaned forward and casually rested a hand on his foot, while she continued to scrutinize his haggard face. "Audubon, what's wrong? What happened?"

His green eyes flickered to her hand. A languid look of pleasure began to cause the tense muscles of his face to relax. "I hoped you'd touch me. I was wondering if I'd imagined the . . . comfort in it. But it's real. You're real."

"I want to help you. If you want me to trust you, then trust me."

"It's not a matter of trust, it's . . . it's habit, I suppose. I've never shared very much about myself with other people. Growing up, it was a necessity. But now . . . well, it's ingrained. I do it instinctively."

"Can't you tell me anything about your business? About your trip to Mexico?"

His somber eyes assessed her for a moment. "I have an adopted son. He works for me. He's twenty-six years old, and he's in trouble with a Mexican businessman who disapproves of a project we've been working on. He disappeared a few days ago, and I've been trying to find him. I have reason to think he's okay and merely hiding until it's safe to call."

"Oh, Audubon, I'm sorry. Your *son*. What are you going to do now?"

"It's too dangerous for me to go back to Mexico—dangerous for my son, that is." Bitterness had entered his voice, and she saw clenched muscles flex in his jaw. "I have to let other people look for him, while I 'supervise' from here, dammit."

"Audubon," Elena said softly, her eyes never leaving his, "Elgiva Kincaid convinced me your business—whatever it is—is nothing illegal. Please tell me she was correct."

"It's not illegal, but it *is* unusual, and if I don't tell you more about it, it's because what you don't know can't hurt you. Another old American saying."

"All right. At least you've told me a little. Perhaps we can trade small secrets until we feel safe enough to share the larger ones."

He smiled, but with a certain hardness in his eyes. A chill ran up her spine as it had the day he took her from the island. Did he intend to use her in some way she didn't yet understand?

Then he destroyed such thoughts by leaning forward and stroking his hand over her hair. "You 'unroll and fluff' fantastically, as Mr. Rex would say."

She dampened her lips and intoned with great drama, "When I'm good, I'm very, very good, and when I'm bad, . . . I frizz." He choked on laughter, and suddenly Elena realized that his laughter meant more to her than anyone else's in her entire life. She *wanted* to please this man, and it was different from wanting to please other people. Wanting to please in the past always had been based on fear . . . or at least the knowledge that she needed someone's goodwill. Wanting to please Audubon was based on the simple, pure need to see him smile.

"When you're good, . . . you're puzzling." He gently brushed the end of her nose with one dusty fingertip. "Where does a Russian find Mae West films?"

"I watched one today," she explained shakily, wondering how the tip of her nose could be such an erotic area. "Bernard and Elgiva and I. But Clarice watched soap musicals."

"Soap musicals?" His eyes squinted, deep lines fanning from the corners as amusement reached them. "You mean soap operas!"

"Whatever."

Leaning his head against the wall, he shut his eyes and smiled, but there was still such anguish in him that it seeped from the edges of his smile like water from a dangerously full dam. Elena caught a soft sound of distress in her throat and slid next to him, her lifelong need to heal anyone who needed her mingling with devotion for him alone.

Murmuring soft words in Russian he didn't need to translate to understand, she unbuttoned his shirt then slid her arms around his waist and hugged him, nuzzling her cheek against the downy mat of dark hair on his chest.

He put his arms around her convulsively, then caressed her back with long, quick strokes of his hands. Each time his fingers moved from the bare skin of her shoulders to the silk-covered region beneath, the change in texture exploded in her nerve endings. She felt dazed with what he was doing to her and loved the hard, masculine textures she absorbed with her own hands as she rubbed slow circles on his spine. "I give comfort, but I also take comfort," she whispered. "Perhaps we can make each other feel better."

"I must have been very, very good to deserve this," he said against her hair. "A whole lifetime of good."

"Some moments are worth a whole lifetime. I have not had many of those, but I'm hoping for more."

"Maybe I can give you one right now." His fingers lingered at the top of her shoulders, then slid under the gown's straps and eased them aside. Her breath shattered as the silk bodice cascaded down her chest, pooling where her breasts pressed hard against his stomach.

Audubon's hands roamed over her neck and shoulders, then trailed down her arms. She tilted her head back and met his kiss, then traded her muted cry of pleasure for the husky purr of his appreciation. Elena knew the slightest shifting of her body would send the gown to her waist. She reveled in the anticipation for a moment, caught in the delicious exploration that her hands were now enjoying along his outer thighs. Then she flexed her torso just enough to let the inevitable follow through.

He broke away from the kiss as their bodies touched again. His tired, worried mood gentled the urgency, but not the deeper bond between them. "You have choices now," he reminded her, drawing his fingertips down her neck, then letting them rest lightly over the pulse point at its base. "And privacy. Your body is your own."

"I know. It's wonderful to share it with you."

With a sigh of satisfaction he pulled her onto his lap and bent his head to her breasts. Elena burned with pleasure as he draped her backward over the sweet, harsh vise of his arm. Every pleasurable sensation in the world shot through her as he tenderly explored her with his mouth.

She clung to his shoulder with one hand and stroked his head with the other, weaving her fingers through his silver hair. Looking down, she watched him in a trance of ecstasy. Her breasts were only average in size, with delicate pink nipples that had never looked large enough to her. But Audubon smiled at their excitement, flirted with them until they were unbearably sensitive, and murmured compliments at their perfection.

Elena lost a smile of wonder in a moan of delight; putting her arms around his head, she shuddered against him and nuzzled his hair. He lifted his head and turned his face against the delicate inner surface of her forearm, placing small kisses in a progression toward her hand. "How do you make flowers bloom?" he whispered, touching the tip of his tongue to her wrist.

"It is . . . a side effect of . . . the energy." Dazed, the cool air enticing her breasts, where his mouth had left the nipples damp and strutted, she carefully shifted herself atop his lap. And she knew when he inhaled sharply and flexed to meet her that she had returned a little of the pleasure he was giving her.

"Does it happen often?" He tilted his head back so that she could dab kisses on his ruddy, parted lips.

"Rarely. Not like it has since I met you." She kissed his chin, his nose, his tired, lined eyes, and the boyish smile that was growing on his mouth. "I could embarrass myself, if I'm not careful. Or frighten someone, like poor Mr. Rex."

Audubon looked up at her with an expression of wonder, making her feel no miracle was impossible between them. "I'll buy you a flower shop. But I insist on being your only customer."

She made a noise that came out sounding like a dove's coo—and they both chuckled. The laughter mingled in another kiss, slow and deep, with small, provocative sounds all its own. She stroked his face, and while one of his hands began to tease her breasts with distracting mischief, the other caught her right hand and brought it to his mouth.

She loved the rough-velvet texture of his lips, especially when they slipped across her palm, then brushed her wrist. The air around her shimmered with anticipation; soon there would be no turning back, but she didn't mind.

"Elena? Elena. What is this?"

Hearing his voice through the pleasant fog of desire, she responded slowly, leaning her head atop his. "Mmmm?"

He rubbed the pad of his thumb over the small bump nestled beside the sinews in her wrist. A rivulet of uncertainty and sorrow crept through her. Straightening, she looked down into his troubled eyes. "It's a birth control implant."

After a startled reappraisal of the bean-sized bump, he asked, "I've read about these, but they're not used in this country."

"It releases hormones regularly, something like taking birth control pills, only there are no pills to take. Once it's placed under the skin, it stays there for two years. It's safe."

"And perfectly acceptable, if it was something you decided for yourself. Was it?"

She looked away. "No."

His shock and anger hummed through her like sympathetic vibrations preceding an earthquake. He gripped her hand in his. "Were you forced—"

"Not forced really, just strongly encouraged." She looked him straight in the eye. "All part of the rules for being a healthy, happy, useful research partner."

"Oh my God."

The disgust in his voice made her chest shudder with the tiny cramps that come from an immediate need to cry out loud with harsh, unrelenting sobs. She subdued the feeling and spoke with a semblance of normalcy. "This is one secret I should never have told."

He cursed under his breath, and though she realized he wasn't cursing at her, but at what had happened to her, still she felt outcast and unsavory, as if she'd told him that she'd been a prostitute. American men were very traditional in some ways, she suddenly recalled being told. Maybe she had the wrong ideas about many things, but she suspected that Audubon was more traditional than not.

But when she pulled her gown straps back into

place and tried to move away, he held her tightly and practically growled at her. "It's all right. I'm just angry. Hell, not just angry, I'm so damned angry I could strangle Kriloff with my bare hands."

It wasn't an idle threat, and she knew it. The compliment of his anger was lost on her as she considered the repulsion in his face and voice. "How many men were there?" he asked.

She froze, disbelieving. "Does it matter?"

He slumped a little, and his voice softened. "No, even one would be too many, considering you had no choice."

There had been only one boy when she turned twenty-one, a boy her own age, and no one had twisted her arm to make her accept him. But after that she had refused to cooperate, until Pavel came along. And because Pavel was one of the psychologists who worked for Kriloff, she had thought he was off-limits. Falling in love with Pavel—who said he loved her too—was rebellion, she thought, until she learned the truth about him.

She was afraid her explanation wouldn't make any difference to Audubon. He was looking at her with something she judged to be pity, the last thing she wanted from him.

"It's not good for us to get so involved, as we did a few minutes ago," she said as cheerfully as she could, while a huge hollow spot grew inside her. "It will make things more complicated when I leave. I don't want to remember you as a lover. I probably won't see you again, so it's smart we stopped when we did."

"Yes. I wasn't thinking when I came up here to see you. I don't know what's going on in my mind right now. But I believe you're right—considering what's probably going to happen, we shouldn't let ourselves be foolish."

She eased away from him, and this time he let her go. "What do you mean, 'What's probably going to happen?' I'm going to get permission to stay in this country, just as soon as Kriloff stops complaining and goes home. Then I'll be free, like everyone else. That's what's going to happen."

"Yes. That's what I meant." He got to his feet and held out a hand. She ignored it and rose by herself, now feeling exposed in the revealing dress. His polite reserve was worse than having strangers study her.

"Good night," she said, and circled around him to the doors of her suite. He stepped forward and opened one of them for her, and she started to tell him that she hated a gallant gesture with no heart behind it. But her eyes caught the miniature plant on the hallway table she'd used as an exercise bar. It was covered in small, starlike pink flowers where there had been nothing but green leaves before he'd come to visit her.

He followed her line of vision, swiveling his head and freezing when he saw the plant. Elena knotted a fist under her throat to keep a sob in check. "Don't worry," she told him, "that won't happen again."

His hard, hurt gaze turned to her, and she absorbed it for as long as she could before she stepped inside the suite and shut the door.

Elena quickly realized that Audubon hadn't told Elgiva or Douglas Kincaid about her unusual powers. She didn't know why he'd keep it secret from his best friends, whom he obviously trusted, but she was glad he had. She didn't know how people on the outside—anyone who hadn't lived at the institute was an 'outsider' to her—would react to her talent. Kriloff had always told her she'd be laughed at and disbelieved, but she was learning that very little he had said was true.

Sitting on the low stone wall of an herb garden a short distance from the main house, she darted a glance past Elgiva, who was picking tiny sprigs off the neat patches of fledgling spring plants. Audubon walked out of the house with Douglas, and Elena's senses went on alert immediately. She heard nothing of what Elgiva went on saying about sage and thyme.

It disturbed her that the mere sight of Audubon, standing next to the brawnier, black-haired Douglas like an elegant white falcon next to a hawk, could make her forget good sense and feel a deep ache of longing. After the traumatic encounter last night, she had to be realistic.

She realized abruptly that Elgiva was waiting for an answer to a question. "I'm sorry. What?"

Elgiva, who was kneeling on a flagstone walkway between patches of mint, stood and shook specks of dirt from the skirt of her dress. "I said, what kind of work would you like to do once you're settled in America. Once you're on your own?"

The question brought a startling image of living somewhere among strangers, free, yes, but completely alone. She stared at Audubon on the manor's back patio, watching him talk intensely with Douglas. To be alone. Never to see Audubon again.

"I've always wanted to own a little bookstore," she told Elgiva distractedly. It was true. She loved the idea of surrounding herself with books and people who loved books. There were so many books that had been unavailable to her in Russia; she could spend years joyfully catching up. But as she continued to watch Audubon, the bookstore idea went from a cozy notion to a wistful one—what if she had nothing but books to love in this large, unknown country?

Elgiva exclaimed softly when she saw her husband and Audubon. "They've finally come out of Audubon's dungeon! Let's go see if they've heard anything new about Kash."

As Elena crossed the lawn beside Elgiva, Audubon raised his head and turned from his conversation. Sliding his hands into the pockets of pearl-gray trousers, his torso rigid under a handsome white pullover with the sleeves pushed up, he took a deceptively casual stance that radiated his own tense mood. She returned his somber attention without blinking, but her nerves vibrated. The material of her cheerful spring dress flowed around her like a separate mood, as deceptive as his own.

Douglas Kincaid, large and brutal in his handsomeness, took Elgiva's hand gently, and, looking troubled, silently drew her with him into the house. Elena's tension soared as she realized she and Audubon were being left alone for some pre-planned discussion about something she felt certain she wasn't going to like.

"Let's take a walk," he said.

She went with him down a pebbled path into a labyrinth of cultivated trees—ornamentals, willows, fruit trees, here and there a gnarled oak, like a giant, sculpted bonsai. It was a shadowy green area, a private jungle dappled with sunlight and sweet with the scent of jasmine. She glanced around hurriedly, wondering if he'd brought her here to see what would bloom.

But she had that under control now, buried under the certainty that there were too few bridges between hers and Audubon's worlds. She stopped in an intimate glen beside a rock-walled basin where a spring bubbled from the ground. He halted also, facing her, his closeness and the intensity of his eyes making her want to take a step backward. But she didn't.

"Tell me," she ordered softly.

"Do you know what the FBI is?"

"Like the KGB, only with nicer suits."

"And nicer rules. They're investigating me, which I expected, but they're getting a little too close for comfort."

"You mean they're trying to decide if you're hiding me?"

"Yes. I've lied. I told them I haven't seen you since the night of the party in Richmond. I could spend a few years of my life eating prison food because of that."

She gasped in dismay, then lifted her chin and

said calmly, "I never asked you to get into trouble on my behalf."

He muttered an ugly-sounding slang word she was glad not to understand. "Your appreciation overwhelms me."

"I never *wanted* to cause you trouble," she amended, her firmness wavering. "You've given me so much . . . the only way I can repay you is by leaving. Now. I'll go somewhere else and call your State Department. No one will ever know that I've been staying here, with you. I'll turn myself in and take the chance they won't let me stay in this country." She looked at her hands, which felt cold. "When I show them my value, however, they'll probably call in all their scientists and have a celebration. Surely then they'll let me stay."

"As a guinea pig."

"What's that?"

"Never mind. I didn't tell you about the FBI to make you feel guilty. I just want to explain why you can't go outside the house anymore. I can't risk someone getting onto the grounds and seeing you. So from now on, you're confined to the house. I'm sorry."

"But what about later? They'll eventually learn I'm here."

"No. I'll work that out when the time arrives."

"Why are you doing so much for me? After last night, I thought you weren't impressed anymore."

His expressive, dark brows stood out like dramatic signals. Now they drew together in support of his ominous expression. "I'm motivated by something a little more important than my groin, Elena. You don't owe me anything because I want to help you. I certainly don't want you to keep acting like a slave, patiently doing whatever you think your 'master' expects."

"Do you think I was being polite last night?"

"Yes, to a degree."

"You ignorant, arrogant . . . you know so little about me, but you make the most insulting assumptions. You've lived your life in such an empty, lonely way, shut off from ordinary people—just like me— but you don't have the faintest understanding of what I was offering you last night. I'm sorry I offered, sorry I expected you to be human."

"I'm *not* human. I'm an Audubon. Be thankful for what that means, because I'm your only hope for getting what you want."

"You don't even know what I want."

"Freedom. Privacy. Independence. To tell the rest of the world, including me, to go take a flying leap."

"You only see the big issues, not the small, quiet, human ones. It's true, what you said, but it's not all." She shut her eyes and saw the world the way she needed for it to be. "I have to be free to give love and respect; to walk into my own house and sit in my own chair, by my own fireplace; to read a book while snuggling in my own bed on a cold winter night. I need to know the book, and the bed, and the comfort, and even the night are mine to do with as I please. Simple goals, but they define me better than grand ones, such as yours."

"When I dream, I dream big," he said gruffly. But when she looked at him, he seemed tired and depressed. "It makes up for a lot of small disappointments."

"And overlooks so many small, private dreams." Her voice trembled with emotion. She ached to touch him, but his aloofness stopped her. His feelings for her were tangled with some larger problem she hadn't discovered yet. She sensed it. She could only be patient, and try to keep from falling more deeply in love with a man who couldn't recognize love even when it made flowers bloom.

Quickly she looked around, then sighed with relief to see no significant change in the greenery. If he didn't understand, she didn't want to humiliate herself again.

"I'd better go inside now," she told him, then added drolly, "Oh, my. I'm being passive and dutiful, like a slave, aren't I?"

"In this case, I approve."

She shot him a challenging look. "I really must make an attempt at being assertive. If I'm to be shut up inside all the time, I *demand* some promises from you."

"Yes?" He drew the word out warily and studied her through slitted eyes.

"Promise to teach me about American customs, so I can fit in."

"All right."

"Including how to attract American men, so I can find boyfriends."

"You'll have no trouble."

*"Promise."*

"All right, my little attack dove, I promise."

"And promise you'll let me visit your private rooms upstairs."

"Why?"

"Because I want to see if you leave dirty socks on the floor. It would be very reassuring to know that in some way you're human."

"You drive a hard bargain. It's a deal. Here's a popular American custom to seal an agreement. Shake." He held out a hand and she grasped it slowly, not certain he wasn't testing her in some way. He squeezed her hand and gave it a gentle tug. "I just wanted to see how much heat the power plant was generating today. Your furnace is cold."

"It was overloaded, so I turned it off."

"Good. You're learning to take care of yourself. Last night you wanted to take care of *me*, but only because it's what you've been trained to do all your life. I don't want that kind of attention."

Trembling with frustration, she managed a grim smile. "Stop making excuses for rejecting me. I won't die because you had a change of heart."

"You misunderstand—" He stopped, looking as frustrated as she felt. "Oh, hell, it's for the best. Change the subject. Let's go back to the house. I'm planning a party in your honor. It'll give you something to look forward to."

Elena stared at him in shock. "You're going to let people know I'm here?"

"Only some very special people."

"People who work for you," she said in dismay. "A fake party."

"People who used to work for me. My friends. I want them to know you, and for you to know them. If anything happened to me, they'd help you."

She grasped his arm. "What do you mean, if anything happened to you?"

Audubon took a startled breath and looked down at her hand on his arm. In a soft voice, he said, "Well, at the moment I might catch on fire."

Elena withdrew her hand, dug her fingertips into her willful, hot palm, but promised silently to singe this fox's silver fur before she was done.

## Six

Audubon was in his downstairs office by dawn. For several hours he read faxes that had come in during the night and talked to his people in various parts of the world. As usual during the past few mornings, his perfectly brewed, custom-blended coffee grew stale in the percolator atop the mahogany étagére near his paper-strewn desk. The chef's magnificent crepes with sausage lay untouched on the gold Audubon family crest of the breakfast china. And his every spare thought was for Elena.

He wanted to reach inside himself and tear out the knot of conflicting emotions that grew larger every day. She had been used for other people's purposes all her life. How would she feel if she knew he might use her too? Kash was in hiding, but Audubon didn't know where; at the moment a dozen of his people were in Mexico trying to locate him before the *wrong* people beat them to it.

If Kash couldn't get out of the situation, Audubon would need help from the State Department. He had cultivated government contacts for years, and even accepted free-lance jobs from the government himself on several occasions. But Kash's situation would take more influence than usual. It would require a bargaining tool: Elena.

Clarice entered his office with a sheaf of notes in

one hand and a prim tilt to her mouth. "If we weren't below ground, you'd be throwing yourself out the nearest window."

Audubon glanced up from his incessant pacing. He held a book on psychic phenomenon in both hands. "Did you give Elena my message?"

"Yes. She'll meet you at the indoor pool in ten minutes."

"Did you tell Bernard to set up everything I asked for?"

"Audubon, if I can run this office for you, I *believe* I can organize a checkers game and lunch for two." Offended, she pivoted on her Italian high heels and marched from the room. He made a note to apologize later. He was edgy not only from worrying about Kash, but because he was balancing on a tightrope between keeping Elena at arm's length and admitting he was desperately in love with her.

She wanted to learn about American customs. Checkers seemed harmless enough, for them both. But he called to Clarice as he left the office, "Did you remember to have Bernard move the geraniums out of the pool house?"

*"Yes."* She shut the office door hard.

Moving the geraniums, which were numerous and nearly ready to bloom, was a wise decision, Audubon knew as soon as he saw Elena. She was sitting on the edge of the indoor pool, looking surreal in the striped shadows of the wooden blinds that covered the glass walls. Her one-piece swimsuit was white, cut high on the hips, but otherwise demure, as if anything could make her supple curves less exciting. He decided to pay Mr. Rex a bonus for picking a suit that was classy but would probably be translucent when wet.

Her eyes, when she looked up at him with the provocative challenge she conveyed so easily, caught the pool's reflected light and were almost as brilliant as the turquoise tile. Their quick, admiring scrutiny and her dismayed smile said she found him and his black swim trunks enormously appealing.

Women had admired him so many times, and dem-
onstrated it in so many ways, that he'd thought
nothing could make him self-conscious. But Elena
did, because he cared so much about her reaction.
He knew his body's imperfections —the sunken scar
just above his left hip, the legs that he considered
too long, with knobby knees and feet that were all
bone and no grace, the cracked rib, from a fist fight
in Morocco, that had healed badly, forming a ridge
that showed on the left side of his chest.

And of course, there was the new scar from the
arrow wound on his right side—more important than
all the others because when her compassionate gaze
went to it, he felt a shiver of awe, remembering what
she'd done to him, giving up her secret to save his
life. He couldn't take advantage of her trust. He
wouldn't let himself think about a future with her,
because the future was so uncertain. To dream about
it and then lose it might shatter all he'd built around
him emotionally throughout his life.

It was too late to make an excuse and cancel lunch,
but he wished he could. The sight of Elena made his
conscience feel raw. His willpower seemed as fragile
as the Japanese rice paper etchings on his library
wall and the Faberge eggs in the display case of his
bedroom. He had filled his home with delicate and
breakable objects in direct contrast to forging his
own unbreakable determination and steely strength.
But now this delicate and breakable woman had
undermined him. Reluctantly he sat down on the
side of the pool and put his feet in the water, as she
had. "Hmmm. Warm. Thank you."

Her mouth curled in droll response. "I never swam
in a giant bathtub before. How decadent."

The remark was a nice shield, but couldn't stop
the accelerated rise and fall of her chest, or the way
her misguided devotion floated to him on the scent
of the gardenia bushes outside the room's glass walls.
Audubon faked a relaxed smile. After all, he was the
one who controlled her future. All he had to do was
keep himself from loving her. "You want to learn

American customs," he taunted mildly. "Then learn to love evil American pleasures."

"Such as?"

As if on cue, Bernard appeared in the open space that led to the manor's central feature, a large vaulted room, filled with massive antiques and oriental pillows. Decorated in shades of warm burgundy, it was a very masculine place of sophisticated comfort. "Are you ready for lunch, Mr. Audubon?"

"Yes. Bring it in, please."

He wheeled a wicker serving cart to a glass-topped table surrounded by upholstered wicker chairs. After setting several covered silver dishes and a silver pitcher frosted with condensation there, he nodded and left. "Come sample an American delicacy," Audubon said, rising and walking to her. He held out a hand, while his eyes went to her delicate cleavage and the streak of sunlight across her worried, mesmerizing face.

His reaction made him very glad that he never wore bikini swim wear—it left nothing to the imagination, which offended his sense of drama, and besides, it showed too much of the scar on his hip. He pretended nonchalance as she took his hand, her fingers dewy and warm. "What luxury?" she asked, drawing her hand away.

Even the hint of her warmth was tormenting. At the table he unveiled their lunch with more impatience than elegance. "Hot dogs."

"Stop your teasing. What are they called, really?"

"I'm not teasing. Eat."

His tense answer silenced her. She repressed all comments about lunch until later, as they lay on their stomachs facing each other on large rafts, with the checkerboard on a float between them. "Why are they called dogs?" she asked, looking at him solemnly with her chin propped on the back of one hand.

"Because they're made of dog meat." He continued setting up the checker pieces, and avoided looking at her. Every time he looked at her he questioned how he could live in this house after she left. He would see her in every room, every hallway—everywhere.

"You like to make fun of me. You're angry. If I could take back what happened between us the other night, I would. It has only made you resent me."

"No. I just don't know what hot dogs are made of. Leftover pieces of pig, I suppose. Who cares? Live dangerously."

"Is that what you've always done—live dangerously."

"Not when I could help it."

"Why would a man who can have anything he wants risk losing it all on mysterious schemes?"

"Not *schemes*. Projects. I help people. Save their lives, even."

"How?"

"By getting them out of problem situations. Just as I helped you."

"For money?"

"Sometimes, if the people are rich and can afford my fee. It depends on the customer."

"And if they can't afford it?"

"If they have a worthy cause, I help them without charge."

"How many people work for you?"

Carefully setting the last checker piece in place, he raised his eyes to hers. "I'll tell you my secrets, if you'll tell yours. What would have happened to you if you'd stayed with Kriloff?"

"I'd have continued participating in his research, of course."

"But what kind of research? I have a mental image of you curing white mice sent over from a cigarette study of severe coughs."

She laughed nervously. "All right, let's play checkers."

"So you're not talking?"

"Neither are you."

"Hmmm." He told her the rules of checkers. She nodded. And then she beat him easily.

"Beginner's luck," he said. So she beat him again. "How do you do it?" he demanded.

"It reminds me of chess. I've played chess since I

was a child. In Russia, everybody plays. By comparison, this game of yours is so simple, I could win it blindfolded." As if to prove that point, she shut her eyes and, as he watched openmouthed, began separating the pieces by color.

Audubon slid off his raft so quickly that he was beside her by the time she opened her eyes in surprise. "This has got to be a trick."

"You only believe in important, fancy miracles? Not funny, simple ones?"

He scrambled the black and red pieces, then snugly cupped his hand over her eyes. "No peeking, this time." She separated the pieces again, red with red, black with black. When he lowered his hand, her eyes gleamed with satisfaction. "Tell me how you did it," he commanded.

"Why should I?" She smiled sweetly.

He turned her raft over, and her yell became a comical gurgle as she disappeared into the pool. When she popped to the surface, she slapped water at him. "Criminal!"

"Brat!" He dove down, circled her legs with his arms, and pulled her under. When he let go of her legs, she deftly raised her feet and hooked them around his hips. As she sprang to the surface her feet scooted down. His trunks went with them.

When he righted himself in the chest-deep water, she was giggling, her hands over her mouth and her face bright red. He gave her a grand scowl. "That was potentially quite painful for me. And definitely undignified."

"I'm sorry, Audubon, I'm sorry. But it's been so long since I've had a chance to be mischievous and have fun. Years, I think. I couldn't resist."

A mental image of her somber past life destroyed his anger and made him want to please her. He thrust his chin forward and eyed her with such fake alarm that she laughed harder. "My trunks are around my ankles. I've tried to be a gentleman to you. I hope you're satisfied with my ungentlemanly predicament."

She wiped her eyes and nodded. "I didn't think

that you'd be too embarrassed. Not a man like you who's probably been naked in many pools with many women. I'm sorry if you don't want to be naked in a pool with me. I don't know why you're so protective."

"So you just want to provoke me."

"I want you to know I don't like being pitied. I want you to understand I'm wise and careful about my feelings. The way I was raised at the institute . . . trained . . . was sad and unfair, but not without dignity. I'm not an emotional invalid. What I was offering you the other night was much more than gratitude for all you've done for me."

The compliment had a direct effect on him, and if she glanced down, she'd get a watery view of a very male response. But Audubon could think only of what would happen if she learned his ulterior motive for helping her. "Maybe I'm not as worldly as you think," he protested.

"A man who doesn't bother to pull up his trunks? Hah." Her expression jaunty, she gazed into the air over his head and busied herself, smoothing her soaked hair back with both hands.

He was right about her swimsuit having a definite see-through quality when it was wet. He doubted that Elena realized how much of a show she was giving him. Her lack of coyness impressed him but made him feel sad, angry, and protective again. He'd never forget that even her most vulnerable, intimate needs had been scheduled like a research experiment. Right now she was stretching her wings, trying to learn how to fly without restraint, and she needed a coach, not a keeper.

He'd play along, from a distance. Crossing his arms over his chest, he said with feigned rebuke, "You're too chicken to take a look at your footwork."

"Too chicken? Why am I always some kind of bird to you?"

"Oh, never mind. After what you did with the checkers, I expect you don't have to look to know what's there."

"But I knew the checkers by"—she hesitated, realized her blunder, and coughed awkwardly—"by touch." Then her expression became impish. "I could learn about you the same way, if you'd like."

He lowered his arms and stared at her. "You can recognize colors by touching them?"

"Not quite. The red pieces had a slightly rougher texture than the black ones, that's all. Something about the difference in paint, I suppose."

"Your sense of touch is that well developed?"

"Yes. It's one of the skills I've perfected over the years, as part of my work with Kriloff. You know, I didn't mind participating in some parts of his research, except that I was never given a choice." Growing somber, she put her hands on the capsized raft that floated nearby. "This white vinyl is a little scratchy." She touched a blue stripe across the raft's headrest. "Smoother." Slowly she brought her attention back to Audubon. Her eyes were anxious. "You're staring at me as if I'm a freak."

"Not a freak. Amazing." Happiness rose in her eyes, warming him with rapt affection.

She began moving toward him. "So I've lost another secret to you. What will you give me in return?"

Audubon forced himself to take a step backward, though every part of him screamed for her fascinating touch, her smile, her future. "Stop, Elena." His request sounded hollow, even to him. The damned swim trunks trapped his feet. A silly kind of fate was at work, he thought grimly. He tried to back up again, but nearly tripped.

She glided up to him and put her hands flat on his chest. "What secret will you give me as payment for mine, Audubon? Something deep in your heart, something from your past, some funny little eccentricity that I'd love? No, not you, not such a private man, certain of his control. I'll have to settle for something you can't hide as easily."

Trembling, she slid her arms around his neck and pressed herself against him. There was nothing between them but her white swimsuit, only millimeters thick . . . and it only made matters worse. Every detail of her lower body was molded to him along with the smooth material, and even her slightest flexing scrubbed him delicately, as if she were stroking him with velvet.

"Silver fox," she whispered, her face flushed with desire and anxious with hope. "You asked me to trust you, and I have. You encouraged me to want you, too, and I have, from the moment we met. Now that you've accomplished so much, why do you tell me to stop?"

*Because I didn't intend to love you. Because I may have to betray you.* Audubon shook his head. He couldn't say either thing to her. "You have a brand new country to explore. You can't imagine how many choices you're going to have about what to see, where to go, and who to share your new life with."

"That's a very unconvincing answer." She trailed her hands down his torso and into the shimmering water. He almost groaned when they smoothed over his sides and back, then lower, only sparing him along the front. There her hands were blocked by her own body, which caressed him in an even more provocative way. "I'm learning to be an American woman. Very bold. I think it's wonderful that American women can simply tell a man they wish to make love to him."

"And you'll have opportunities with any other man you want."

"But wanting is not the same as wanting to *make love*. You're quivering, Audubon." Her voice broke with emotion. It was the barest of whispers now, her breath feathering his lips as she raised her face closer to his. "No other woman could tell that you are. You won't even admit it, yourself. But I know. I feel it in my fingertips. Here. And here. Oh, Audubon, touching you is like living inside your world. All your mysteries are at my fingertips. Share them, please. *Please.*"

He had been born with a crystal dome around him, setting him apart from other people, displaying him like a rare museum piece, a symbol of so many things—his notorious heritage, his wealth, his ideals. No one had ever broken through it until now. Suddenly she was with him, heating him from the inside out, and his mind went blank with the magnificence of being part of her.

Audubon put his arms around her gently, brushed kisses across her face and tasted the small, happy sounds she made when he reached her mouth. He drew her to him in an embrace so sensual that no movement was necessary, and they stood still, their heads on each other's shoulders, hands unmoving, only the water stroking the single, melded entity they had become.

"You do not take," she murmured in awe. "You give. You give when it would be easy just to take."

He shut his eyes, troubled by what she'd think if she knew he had already planned how he'd leak information about her to the State Department—not telling where she was, but simply letting them know that she was something much more unusual than a secretary to Dr. Gregori Kriloff. Once her powers were known, she'd never be free in the way she wanted. But he would have a major bargaining tool for getting help for Kash, if it was needed.

"I want your life to be everything you want it to be," he said. "But I'm more selfish than you think." He dropped a kiss on her shoulder, then bit the spot gently, as if warning her.

She inhaled sharply, arching inside the arm he'd circled around her waist. Her head came up as he cinched her tighter against him, and her breath feathered rapidly against the side of his neck. "I know you intend to use me in some way."

For a moment, shocked, he said nothing. Then he turned his head and caught the tip of her earlobe between his teeth, raked it painlessly, and heard her soft, helpless gasp again. Driven by regret and frustration, he was helpless, himself. "What an insulting thing to say. Why do you trust me, if you suspect my motives?"

"Because I don't think I'm mistaken about you."
She hugged him fiercely, and put her head on his
shoulder again. "I feel great gentleness in you, and
I've seen the respect people give you—there's no fear
in it. You've earned the kind of loyalty that only
comes to those who are honorable." She paused. "I'd
recognize the opposite kind easily. I've known it all
my life."

He told himself her words were flattery—sincere,
but uninformed flattery—and they shouldn't affect
him. But they burst inside him like flowers, blooming profusely, filling him with bright colors of desire, emotion, and hope.

In the dim haze of passion and despair, he didn't
hear the first hushed chime of the house alarm
system. But the second pierced him like a bullet. By
the time he set her away and lifted his trunks to the
surface with his foot, a technique borrowed from his
soccer-playing days in one of Virginia's finest military academies, Bernard was standing in the doorway to the great room, a portable phone in one
hand.

"Michael says we have most unusual visitors on
their way up the drive."

*Most unusual.* The standard wording Bernard used
in front of guests. Dangerous visitors. Anyone who
had gotten past the guard at the gate without
Audubon's permission must have a search warrant.

And there was only one reason for it. Elena.

"Entertain our guests until I change clothes," Audubon called calmly. Bernard nodded and left. If he
had glimpsed Audubon's nakedness under the water, he gave no sign.

Sliding to the side of the pool, Audubon forced
himself to move with unhurried ease, but adrenaline poured into his bloodstream. Elena met his reassuring gaze with a starkly fearful one. She knew.
Dammit, she was too sensitive. She knew something was very wrong.

Audubon shook his head at her. "Relax. Why don't
you get yourself a towel and dry off?" Reaching for

the pool's edge beside his head, he tossed the swim trunks on the tile then winked at her. "Are you really going to stand there and stare at me while I get out? I'll blush, I swear." His husky teasing only made her nod woodenly. All her fears about being found and sent back to Kriloff had jelled in the horrified expression on her face. "Elena," he said softly, keeping his urgency hidden, "trust me."

That galvanized her. Nodding again, this time firmly, she swam to the pool's shallow edge and climbed out, then ran to the white towel draped on a wicker couch and wrapped it around her like a skirt. By that time he had put on his swim trunks and vaulted to his feet. "Let's take a walk, wet dove." He held out his hand.

She trotted to him and grasped it hard. Both of them dripping water on the hardwood floors and thick imported rugs, they walked through the great room. "Who do you think's come to look for me?"

"Probably the FBI."

"What will they do?"

"Ask me a number of insulting questions and search the house."

He led her into the central hall past Italian porcelain vases as tall as their heads, and paintings worth more than most homes. He had an impractical, illogical urge to pile everything outside the main entrance and set fire to it, as a blockade. Riches up in smoke, easily forgotten, for the protection of a loved one. Great-great-great-uncle Zeodorus Audubon had done something similar during the Civil War, to save his invalid wife from being evicted by Yankee troops.

"Where are we going?" Elena asked, unaware that once again an Audubon was intent on saving his heart's blood from Yankees. She probably didn't even know what Yankees were. And the FBI types were probably Southerners, anyway, men named Billy Frank and Tommy Lee, and . . .

He was losing his mind. The supercool icing system around his nerves had never threatened to shut down before. *You've never been in love like this before.*

"I'm taking you to my dungeon," he said with a short, smooth laugh, then raised her hand and kissed it. They entered his paneled study, where polo trophies glinted in sterling silver grandeur on the fireplace mantel.

"Won't they look in your 'dungeon' as well?" she asked as he led her through a door on the other side of the study.

"They don't know it exists. And they have no way of finding out." The smaller room, with thick, paisley-print drapes hiding the windows, was Clarice's office. But she was standing by an opening in the paneled wall, smoothing her gray chignon with one hand and flicking a bit of lint off her white coatdress with another. As Audubon and Elena halted, Clarice smiled at her but shot a furtive, worried look at Audubon. "This is no place for a swim, Chief."

He chuckled at their pool attire and dripping bodies. "We're looking for the secretarial pool."

"Phew-wee. Put that joke in the sun and let it stink."

"Stop speaking in a secret code," Elena begged softly, looking from Clarice to Audubon with blue eyes gone nearly violet with concern. "Please."

He let go of her hand and quickly put his arm around her in a hug. "It's no secret code, I promise. Follow Clarice downstairs and don't worry about a thing. I'll be down to get you when it's safe."

"I hope you like root beer and marshmallows," Clarice commented. "Because that's what you and I are going to be stuck with to munch on until Bernard has time to come down with something more appetizing."

"I'm sure they'll be fine—whatever these root beers are," Elena told her. She faced Audubon and grasped his arms. "In my country, when government men come to people's homes, it's very bad."

"Here we only worry if they're from Animal Control. Last month I was ticketed for letting my hot dogs run free."

"What?"

"Shhh. Nothing's going to happen to you."

"I'm worried about *you*."

If Clarice hadn't been observing with her motherly brown eyes, he would have picked Elena up and kissed her. Instead he merely smiled. "Go downstairs, now. I'll see you soon."

She looked at him stoically as she entered the stairwell with Clarice. When the panel slid shut behind them, Audubon felt he had just sealed all his treasures in a vault.


Occasionally from somewhere in the mansion would come the slap of a heavy teak door being shut, the muffled rhythm of men's feet on hardwood floors, the low voices of a dozen FBI agents communicating with each other through walkie-talkies. Audubon half-listened to the sounds of agents rummaging through his home, while he sat, now dressed in a pale blue pullover and tan slacks, behind the massive desk in his study. He lounged in a tall, upholstered chair with his legs crossed, and drank a cup of tea.

"You have my secretary, and I intend to get her back," Gregori Kriloff said with gruff authority, so scowling and bushy-browed that Audubon was constantly reminded of large, portly terriers with overgrown fur. Beside Kriloff's armchair sat a handsomely suited, but very nervous State Department official, and the FBI man in charge of the case. The FBI agent kept staring at Audubon with cold, competitive envy.

"I saw her once at the Parklane Hotel reception almost two weeks ago," Audubon said again. "She wasn't exactly an attractive woman, and between her shyness and her lack of English, we could barely communicate. Why in the world would I want to help her defect? Or, as you even more bizarrely suggest, kidnap her? I assure you, Doctor, my taste in women runs to statuesque brunettes with money and careers. Someone in my own class, certainly, not a drab little blonde impersonating a rock." He sipped his tea from a china cup. "An Audubon get involved with a Russian woman? My ancestors would be turning in their graves."

"You sly bastard, I've learned all about you," Kriloff retorted. "You and your private little 'James Bond' organization, running about the world rescuing people, trampling on the toes of legitimate police and military personnel—"

"Actually, Mr. Audubon has often cooperated with us," the State Department man interjected, clearing his throat. "He's been very helpful."

"When he doesn't stick his face into official business," the FBI man amended.

Audubon smiled at all three men. "I'm just a high-priced, state-of-the-art security expert, gentlemen, who offers his services to a wide range of clients. I have a business license, if you'd care to see it."

"I care to see Elena Petrovic," Kriloff said. "I know that she went to an island off the coast of this state, and worked briefly for a farmer-woman there. A man who fit your description asked the farmer questions about her new employee—Elena—and shortly thereafter Elena disappeared from the island. The farmer had a note from Elena, saying that she'd left with a passing fisherman to find work elsewhere. But the handwriting was *not* Elena's."

"None of which means a thing to me," Audubon said smoothly. "But I'm curious—why is your secretary so important? I mean, if she wants to defect so badly, why do you care? Frankly, she didn't seem either bright or capable of efficiency to me."

Kriloff leaned forward, dark eyes burning with impatience. "Listen to me. I raised her. She's like a daughter to me, but she's a frail, troubled young woman. You can't believe anything she tells you. She's quite irresponsible and has a vivid imagination." His voice dropped, becoming patient and fatherly, as if he felt sorry for Audubon. "She has very little control of herself around men. She's had dozens of sexual partners. *Dozens*. Don't take her seriously if she tries to appeal to your vanity. She would be using you."

Audubon lifted his teacup in a salute. "Here's to the Russian nymphomaniac, wherever she may be." He thought about smashing the cup into the doctor's face, but banished the image. It was too tempting.

"She will leave you when she has an opportunity without a backward glance."

"No, I'll lock her in my bedroom and beg her to appeal to my vanity."

"Make jokes, Mr. Audubon, but I will get her back. For her own good. She cannot roam the world unsupervised. She's not suited for it. In fact, it might destroy her."

"Now that's intriguing. Tell me more."

"You'll see, if you haven't already."

Audubon set his teacup down and sighed grandly. "I'm innocent, Doctor."

Kriloff spat out Russian words, then rose and walked out of the study, head up and dignity intact. He was not a harmless enemy, Audubon admitted distractedly, while still mentally playing back some of the things the doctor had said. He discounted the obvious lies and honed in on the hints of truth.

She'd had dozens of *lovers*? No. But from what she'd said there was no doubt that she'd been pressured to have relationships as part of the doctor's comprehensive study of paranormals. It had not been her own choice, or pleasure, and he suspected that it had been much worse than she'd led him to believe. Whether that made her feelings for him a vulnerable mixture of new-found freedom, gratitude, and emotional naïveté, he didn't know yet. He only knew he cherished her affection and passion.

*She can't roam the world unsupervised. It might destroy her.* That comment stayed in his mind, too, putting an ominous chill on his skin. He had to draw back from her, maintain his distance, and understand the secrets she guarded as closely as he guarded his own.

And hope they didn't destroy each other.

His office was sumptuous and neat—there were no papers on the massive desk to reveal anything about his work, and few personal objects to intrigue her. Except the photos. She was so worried about what might be happening upstairs that she leapt at any distraction.

The photographs were at least twenty-five years old. Clarice pulled them from behind a row of encyclopedias on the floor-to-ceiling bookcases. She didn't explain the lack of more recent photos or their strange location, and by now Elena knew better than to expect anyone but Audubon to discuss his family in detail, so she didn't ask.

But she didn't need to ask to know the power of the people in the photographs. The family's wealth leapt out at her from their elegant clothes and proud faces against a fabulous white mansion with tall columns across the front, from a sailing yacht bathed in ocean and sky, from sleek thoroughbreds outfitted for the hunt. Only Audubon's sister, just a child, had looked at the camera with a hint of a smile.

"What's going on here? Photo day in the bunker?"

Audubon, in the flesh, didn't smile at all. A family tradition had caught up with him. She rushed to him, relieved that no one had taken him away. He answered her frantic questions with maddeningly vague answers. Of course they were still looking for her. Of course they suspected him. No, they had no proof.

"What did Kriloff say?"

"That you're just a secretary. He wants you back because he feels responsible for you. He raised you." A tiny gleam of humor lightened Audubon's somber expression. "That you're one hot mama, when it comes to men. He warned me not to be caught in your sultry spell, because you're fickle and fast."

Clarice tactfully left the office. Elena gaped at him. It was so outrageous, she had to swallow a yelp of fury. "I never wanted to be a hot mother! I did what I was told!"

"Calm down. I don't doubt you."

"But I'm not sure if what you understand is accurate. What do you think? Do you believe I was some kind of—"

"Elena, forget that. He's bluffing, and it's not important. He said something else that is important, though. He said you can't survive in the outside world. I think he was hinting about your gift. What could he have meant?"

She said a little too quickly, "What nonsense. He's fluffing again, of course."

"Bluffing, Elena?" He looked at her with one dark brow arched, and the lock of silver hair that had fallen across the lined, weathered skin of his forehead seemed to her like a badge of wisdom, won in shrewd battles with far more skilled opponents than she. He stared at her grimly, waiting.

"Audubon, I am obviously surviving in the outside world. You can see."

"I'm asking you to tell me the truth. Do you have a problem I need to know about?"

She shook her head. She would learn to deal with it. He didn't need to know. "No problem."

"Elena," he said with warning.

"I said, *There's no problem.*"

Taking her by the shoulders, he studied her face with unrelenting intensity. She held firm, but her stomach knotted. With a slow hiss of dismay he reached his verdict. "You're hiding something damned important to you. This is one time you and I aren't going to play games. Tell me—right now!—what Kriloff meant."

"He meant to see if you're a fool who'll believe anything he says. Of course he wants you to think I belong back at the institute!"

"I'd never believe him. I want to believe you."

"Then believe what I say about this. Stop digging

into my life. Just help me, and don't ask so many questions."

"That's not a fair trade, Elena."

"Oh? Are we bargaining for my future now?"

"You may be throwing it away, if you don't cooperate."

"Is that a threat?"

He lifted her to her toes, not hurting her with the grip on her arms, but putting her off balance so she sank her hands into his shirtfront for support. The white towel fell from around her waist, and she felt too vulnerable, hanging there in his powerful hands, with him fully clothed and her dressed in nothing but the white swimsuit.

Audubon looked down at her body, making the examination slow and intense. "You've offered to give yourself, and I could have taken you—just as you said when we were in the pool. Why haven't I, do you think?"

"I really don't know."

"Because I don't want to hurt you. So don't accuse me of making threats."

"How would it hurt me to make love with you?"

"When this trouble blows over, you want to be free. You deserve to be. And I don't want to complicate your life. I'm not the right man for you. I'm away most of the time on business. I'm totally involved in my work. I don't have anything to give to an important relationship."

He let her down, let her get her feet firmly planted on the floor. In more ways than one. She looked at him with tortured acceptance. He didn't want to be bothered with her. It was stunning to think she'd misunderstood all the passion between them. Was she that inexperienced with human emotion, compared to his sophisticated self?

Or was she just too odd and too foreign, too awkward and untrained in his country's ways? A new thought chilled her. She wasn't in his class. Audubon needed a woman at his own level: Blue-blooded, wealthy, American.

"I'll go back to my suite now, if it's safe," she said in a hushed, angry tone.

"You won't tell me what Kriloff meant?"

She stared at him evenly, then bent, retrieved her towel, and wrapped it around her waist without answering. "How soon do you think I can leave here?"

"And go where?"

"Wherever I like." She held his gaze. "Isn't that the whole point?"

"I'm out of answers at the moment."

"No, you're only thinking up new tactics. You're as manipulative as Kriloff."

The muscles in his jaw tightened, and his eyes took on the shuttered, ominous coldness she'd seen before. He went to his desk and sat down with smooth grace in a tall swivel chair. "Don't forget the party in your honor tomorrow night."

"A party? No. A show. I'm to be on display for your coconspirators."

"And their spouses."

"Should I tell them why I'm important to you? I could perform party tricks, if you'd like."

He punched a button on a phone intercom. "Clarice, show Elena back to the main floor, please." Leaning back in his chair, he steepled his fingers under his chin and watched her. In a low, hard voice he said, "You have no idea why you're important to me."

"I intend to find out." She pivoted and left his office, barefoot, still damp from the pool, one hand pinning her impromptu skirt together at her hip. She felt her hopes were just as likely to fall as the towel.

# *Seven*

At two A.M. Elena roamed Audubon's house, drawn farther and farther from her suite until she reached the destination that had taunted her for hours. Barefoot, wearing only a gown and robe, she padded into the large, dark vestibule outside Audubon's private wing. Stopping there in tormented silence, she wondered if he could see her because of some hidden camera, if he might be watching her make a fool of herself. She went to the heavily carved double doors and flattened her hands on them, wishing that the wood could talk. He was just inside, but so far away.

She was still shaken by Kriloff's visit and the anger between her and Audubon. She had always had trouble with insomnia, because she had learned so early in life to bury her fears and fantasies. So they came out at night in vivid and sometimes frightening dreams, and even when there were no dreams, her body couldn't slough off the tension. At the institute she'd grown accustomed to napping rather than sleeping, and often spent large portions of the night either reading, practicing ballet, or listening to pop music on her tinny-sounding record player.

Giving a frown of self-rebuke, she turned and, hugging herself, head down in thought, walked back toward the main hall. The doors to his suite opened with a sudden swoosh of wood brushing over soft

rugs. She reeled, startled. He stood in the opening, one hand on each door, the light shadowing
him. The man belonged in the theater. His natural
sense of drama was breathtaking.

He wore black pajama bottoms and nothing else,
and there was only a small brass lamp shining in
the darkened, vague area behind him, but he didn't
have the disheveled look of a man who'd been in
bed. "Is something wrong?" he asked brusquely.

"No. I was just exploring. I can't sleep."

"Guilt is a terrible bedmate."

'So you can't sleep, either, I assume."

He held out a hand and coaxed in a fluid, provocative voice, "Come and let me give you the after-hours
tour. You said you wanted to see my private rooms."

She knew what he wanted—information—and that
he wasn't above tantalizing her to change her mood.
"I'd like the tour, but I can't pay the price of
admission."

"Oh, it's free."

"I know you too well, Audubon. You are nervous."

"Calm me down, then. Keep me company for a few
minutes. See what you think of the fox's den. Or are
you the nervous one? An honest change of heart is
nothing to feel anxious about. Come in and unbur-
den yourself of secrets."

"No anxiety. No change of heart. My tour, please."
She entered his suite as he stepped aside and bowed,
sweeping one arm toward the intimate shadows.
Elena clasped her hands behind her back and glanced
around casually, while the atmosphere seeped into
her blood with disarming power and nearly made
her dizzy.

"There's something about Victorian style that ap-
peals to the sensual side of human nature," Audubon
said, shutting the doors so quickly that the well-
oiled snap of the heavy latch echoed in her pulse.
The small room, a parlor or library, had an arched
doorway on the other side—her escape route? Hardly.
It led only to the rest of his private world.

Except for the contemporary news magazines and

newspapers scattered among the tapestry pillows of a curving, gilt-edged sofa, or the ebony armoire open to reveal an array of television and stereo equipment on its shelves, the room belonged in the last century.

"You see," Audubon continued, strolling across richly patterned rugs that nearly hid the varnished floor, "the Victorian era was very straight-laced, even repressed." He went to a window covered in heavy, emerald drapes and lifted a braided pull rope with a tasseled end. "Velvet drapes. A satin rope. I think Victorian men and women poured all that hidden passion into provocative decorations. The textures are incredible. Come and feel them."

She floated forward, her hands trembling behind her, her common sense telling her that she knew exactly what he was trying to do and wasn't fooled. Tempted, but not fooled.

"Yes, very nice," she commented, scrubbing her knuckles along the curtains, then poking the thick rope with a fingernail.

"I designed these rooms to bring out the worst in my nature."

"Oh? Are there secret panels everywhere?"

He laughed softly, the sound so plush, she could have lost herself in the sultry depth, as if it were the pillows, the rugs, the drapes. She could lose her control in his voice, in this place. He took her arm and led her toward the inner door. "My hedonistic nature. Under my busy, efficient facade is the heart of a centaur. I was really meant to lounge about naked on huge pillows with a garland of flowers on my head, eating grapes from the hands of a beautiful, adoring woman. Naked also, of course."

"Centaur. Isn't that a nasty, half-goat creature?"

"Half horse, my dear, cruel dove, half horse."

He guided her with the disarming pressure of his fingers and palm on the back of her arm, and her thin silk robe did nothing to hamper the effect. Her breath stopped in her throat as they walked silently down a cozy hall lit by prismed wall sconces. "My bedroom," he said, gesturing to a wide entrance framed in carved wood. He reached past her with one arm, curving his body around her as he flicked a light switch on the crystal lamp atop a table inside the room. His scent and warmth enveloped her; his broad, furry chest was so close, it brushed her shoulder.

Elena's knees went weak as she studied a room even more overstuffed with texture and emotion. The bed against the center wall was enormous and black-lacquered, the headboard, footboard, and tall posts designed in a combination of straight and curving patterns. Male and female. And on the mattress was a jumble of scarlet-and-gold brocade and shimmering ivory silk sheets, with large pillows scattered among the turbulence.

"I don't allow my bed to be made," he purred. "It's part of my private delight in laziness."

That bed was hardly a place to be lazy. Drained, delighted, and unable to budge from too much indulgence, perhaps, but not lazy. And if she came within caressing distance of the covers, with Audubon's taunting, confident sensuality to push her over the edge . . . she'd dissolve into his arms and tell him anything he wanted to know, then beg him to do with her as he pleased.

She backed away and glanced about the hall, her head swimming from desperation. "Next?"

She shot a quick look at him and saw that his large, thickly lashed eyes were watching her with determined patience, the challenge barely concealed. "My dressing room."

They moved farther down the hall. Again he reached past her into a dark entrance. The scent of fine colognes and fabrics added to the basic male appeal of the scent of his skin. The soft overhead light came on.

She looked distractedly into a wonderland of mirrors, closets, racks of clothes, racks of shoes, shelves filled with hats, open drawers spilling linen handkerchiefs and even . . . a black wicker clothes hamper in one corner, where a single black sock dangled, caught under the lid. "You see," he said beside her, his voice an amused rumble. "A dirty sock, just as you hoped to find. Aren't you reassured that I'm human, vulnerable?"

Tears rose in her eyes. "I wish it was that simple. I would love to be reassured. I would love to—" Her voice broke. "But I'm only making a fool of myself. Forgive me for coming here tonight. I must be losing my mind."

"Elena," he said hoarsely, and it was a stark change from the teasing, the seduction, the charade. The sorrow in it broke her control, and she turned blindly, intent on leaving before recklessness overtook her. He caught her arms from behind. "Elena, there are a thousand things I wish I could say and do to make you happy."

She twisted her head to look at him, and he made her lean against his bare chest in the process. She bit back a soft moan and said, "But none of them suits your plans—whatever those are."

"I won't hurt you. I swear I won't."

Being cared for had never been so tormenting. He didn't want to hurt her? But he didn't want to love her, either, or share any part of his life with her. How badly he had hurt her already, without knowing it.

"Please let go of me. Please."

He dropped his hands but didn't move away. She was forced to make the hard step out of his reach, when the greedy, reckless part of her soul was demanding that she stay, if he'd have her. He didn't even want to take her to bed, for fear of hurting her, he'd said. She was some kind of emotional cripple to him.

She walked swiftly up the hall, checking the tie of her robe, pulling the creamy lapels closer over her breasts. She felt as if he'd made love to her, and it seemed strange to be dressed. He strode after her, right on her heels, to the front room. Balanced on the balls of her feet for escape, she stopped by the double doors. "Good night." She looked up into his angry, sad, hypnotizing green eyes, and nearly sagged against him. "I know you thought I'd admit some fascinating secret. I apologize for wasting your time."

"If you don't leave, we'll be in bed together within the next five minutes, and neither of us will care if making love is an unwise thing to do."

Knowing what he said was true, she dragged the doors open and stumbled, in her hurry to leave. He caught her elbow to keep her from falling. "Take care, dove." He sounded miserable. She pulled away and kept going without looking back, almost running down the big, empty hall.

She sat in front of the vanity mirror in her bathroom, trying to apply the eye makeup Mr. Rex had given her. Her hand shook, and she finally laid the mauve pencil down in defeat.

She hadn't seen Audubon all day. In fact, she'd had to stay in her suite and play cards with Elgiva Kincaid until the florist and caterer had made their deliveries for the party. The party was in her honor. The party that was nothing more than an excuse for Audubon to present her to his curious cronies. They didn't know about her unusual abilities, so they were probably baffled over their friend's interest in hiding an average, ordinary Russian secretary. Maybe they thought he had lost a few of his expensive marbles, even.

Cronies. Lost marbles. She was learning American slang. And learning how to dress like a wealthy American woman. She looked over at the long, white taffeta skirt and fitted black jacket that waited on quilted hangers hooked over the door. The jacket had real onyx buttons up the back, and intricate gold piping swirled up the front in abstract patterns.

From her black patent shoes to her new hairstyle she'd be fashionable, just like the women in Audubon's social set, and no one at this party would gawk at her ugliness. But that didn't mean she'd impress anyone with her social skills. She didn't have any social skills.

A few minutes later, Elgiva came to the suite and rescued her from the makeup chores. Elgiva made no claim to glamour, but she achieved it anyway. Her tall, curvaceous body was swathed in soft blue satin, sapphires gleaming in her ears, her mane of auburn hair twisted up in a loose, wispy style.

She plunked down next to Elena on the vanity bench and sang under her breath as she dabbed makeup on Elena's closed eyes. "My Douglas and I are pregnant! I just told him today."

Elena gave her a hug. "I'm very happy for you, my friend."

"I'm 36 years old, you see, and I never had children with my first husband. Twelve years—I was sure it was my fault." Elgiva's expression grew wistful. "When Douglas and I married I didna' know if we'd have any bairns together, and I told him so. The lovely man promised it didna' matter, but a year ago we decided to try. I was beginning to be afraid nothing would happen." She patted her abdomen. "But it *did* happen. Two months. The wee babe is two months along. I waited until it was absolutely certain before I told Douglas."

"He's very happy, I'm sure."

"Happy?" Elgiva laughed with pure joy. "There's no word to describe how happy we are."

"I'd like to have children someday. And a husband. I suppose anything's possible, now that I'm free." But she didn't feel very free, or like marrying anyone. Other than Audubon. It was alarming how much that daydream had taken hold of her thoughts lately.

Elgiva put an arm around her. "You look so sad. You do love Audubon, I can see it."

Elena shuddered with defeat. She could tell Elgiva, at least. "Yes. Isn't that something? I waited a lifetime to find him, and he doesn't want me."

"Nooo, or I must be blind, and Douglas too. And

just wait until the old gang sees Audubon with you. Ask them if they've ever witnessed the like before."

"Who are they, really? Audubon is in the business of rescuing people—he told me about it. It's safe for you to explain a little."

Elgiva hesitated, then sighed. "The crew you'll meet are all retired agents of his. All of them had backgrounds in the military or the police before coming to work for Audubon. They worked for him for many years, but none are older than himself. It's a tough business, and the ones you'll meet tonight were wise to let fresh people take their places. Though Audubon has never forgiven a one of them for leaving him."

"Why?"

"They all went off and got married. He will no' have a married agent working for him—it's his rule. The work's too demanding and too dangerous, he says. And too confidential. But it goads him that his old friends left him. He's like a race horse who's still racing when the others are enjoying themselves in the pasture."

"I'll make them like me."

"They'll like you just as you are, lass. Relax."

Elena smiled as if it was that simple, but she already had a plan. She looked at her slender, tapering hands, pretty by most standards, but nothing special. Tonight, using every control technique she had learned over the years, she'd focus the wonderful power that poured through them. She'd win the friendship of Audubon's elite circle and prove to him she was worthy. She could hurt herself if she wasn't careful, but taking risks was what freedom—and love—was all about.

He could only think about Elena, about bringing her downstairs to meet his guests, about making certain they liked her. Not that he doubted their loyalty; each of the dozen men he'd invited here tonight would gladly help her if anything happened to him. But he wanted them to see her as the strong, courageous, beautiful person she was. None of them knew about her unique gift, and didn't need to know, right now. Maybe later, if the situation became desperate.

But he wanted to preserve her secret, the secret only he and she shared. The men here tonight, and their remarkable wives, only needed to know that Elena was his treasure, even if he didn't admit she was also his love.

They would have trouble believing Audubon could feel love—blinding, sentimental love. It would have made them choke on their champagne, if he announced it. He wasn't about to. Better that no one knew, considering how dim the future was. They had heard about Kash, that he was still missing. He was another of the reasons they'd traveled from their far-flung homes to see Audubon.

A glowing amber sunset had just disappeared into the horizon when the last of the guests arrived in limousines from the airport. In the great room that opened into the pool house they talked in small groups, enjoying their reunion the way old soldiers enjoy rehashing battles, the wives listening patiently, as Bernard replenished trays of hors d'oeuvres and tended bar.

Audubon picked a rosebud from an arrangement on a sofa table, tucked it in the lapel of his black tuxedo, then realized his mistake and hurriedly laid the rosebud aside. He stared at vases filled with flowers all over the room. Good Lord, a disaster. The buds would burst into bloom; the blooms would widen until they looked as if they'd been mashed flat.

No. He'd forgotten—Elena had come to her senses. That had been clear last night. She hadn't been swayed by him. She'd run. He'd let her go. Perhaps the flowers wouldn't go wild tonight.

Depressed, he moved among his guests with the detached graciousness they knew well and didn't misinterpret as arrogance. They understood he was happy to see them and welcomed them all. His home had been their headquarters for many years, and each of them had worked there, even lived there briefly, at times.

The former agents were an entirely male group from the old days, and Audubon was always a little sorry he hadn't begun hiring women until the past few years. He'd feared he'd worry about women agents more than men—an inescapable character trait of his, part masculine instinct, part upbringing. But the women he now employed had added a valuable perspective to the work; women were better negotiators, more likely to settle problems with words instead of force.

Or, in the case of Elena, likely to settle problems with a devastating *hands-on* power. He eyed the group with a startling new perspective: For the first time, he was glad they were all married and very much in love with their wives. His surge of possessiveness toward Elena would have caused tension, if there'd been an eligible bachelor among the group.

Elgiva entered the room, went to Douglas, who had not worked for Audubon but was essentially his partner, and he swept her up in his arms and kissed her several times while she laughed. Audubon had been waiting eagerly for Elgiva to come downstairs; now he had to force himself not to hurry over to her and demand information on Elena's readiness.

Douglas was grinning with delight at everyone, even Audubon. Audubon's mood snapped and he strode over to them. Babies. Married people. Loneliness. Elena. "What is she doing up there, plotting the next Russian Revolution? Is anything wrong?"

Elgiva gave him an exasperated look from her happy place in Douglas's arms. "She's ready. I told her you'd be coming up to escort her." He nodded and pivoted to leave, but she grasped his sleeve. "Audubon, she's so shy that she's—I could swear that she's *vibrating*. Oh, I know it sounds foolish, but she seems so nervous, no, not nervous, exactly. Agh! Go see for yourself. Maybe she's coming down with a fever. When I helped her put on her makeup, her face felt hot. You ask her if she's all right, will you?"

He didn't have to ask. He knew what was happening—the energy, the heat—but he didn't know why. If she was gearing up for something, he doubted it had to do with him.

Elena had the suite door open before he finished knocking. She almost winced at the surprised look he gave her. She hadn't started this important evening on a very sophisticated note, flinging the door back in her anxiety to see him.

"Very, very nice," he said after a moment, and she realized that he was referring to the way she looked, as his gaze traveled down the short black bodice with its fitted sleeves and the flowing white skirt. He brushed a fingertip across the braided gold design that curled from the stand-up collar down the jacket's front. "It has a certain stern, Victorian quality." His voice became husky and sly. "But the textures hint at something sensual, perhaps even wild, underneath."

His hand dropped to his side. She got herself under control and gave his devastating body, in its devastating black tuxedo, a cool appraisal. Finally her gaze halted on his lapel. "No boutonniere? I told you your flowers would be safe around me."

"Can you really turn the power off whenever you want?"

She smoothed her skirt and looked away, the danger too close. He mustn't worry about her and believe Kriloff's dark hints. "I'm not a toaster, Audubon. I don't have a switch. But I'm quite capable of taking care of myself *and* my gift."

"Hmmm, so defensive. Well, come along. Your party is waiting." He shut the door for her as she stepped into the hall, then held out his arm. She lightly tucked her hand around his elbow. She looked away from his intense scrutiny and concentrated on maintaining her reserve.

"Very good," he murmured as they reached the wide staircase to the main floor. "You've wrapped a nice little shield around it, haven't you?" He sounded more angry than pleased.

"For now. Perhaps I'll start shooting off invisible lightning bolts when I meet your friends. Are any of them unmarried?"

"I'm afraid not."

They were halfway down the long staircase. He halted, turned toward her, and said with unflustered command, "We'll find you a suitable man, but not tonight."

"We? Is that the royal 'we,' your lordship?"

"You and I. You asked me to teach you how to attract American men. But not tonight."

She swallowed a painful little sound and stared straight ahead. She'd asked for that, provoked it. But was he serious? "I'll try not to be a temptress."

"A wise decision. The wives will appreciate it."

Wrapped in brittle silence, they went downstairs and through the opulent central hall to the back of the house. When they entered the great room with all its grandeur, two dozen of the most elegant men and women she'd ever seen stopped their conversations and studied her with what seemed like shocked expressions. Her legs turned rubbery. She gripped Audubon's arm hard.

Yes, she'd have to give dangerously close to everything, to impress these friends of his.

When Audubon guided her into their midst and began introducing each to her, their names were a blur. She focused on their handshakes, and the puzzled smiles that followed told her they'd felt the comforting warmth, the reaching out. It was the same for the women as the men, a friendly little *zap* of energy, just enough to make them wonder if they'd really felt it, and be curious.

But there was one man with traces of hideous scars on a kind, handsome face, and the scars caught her off guard. Before she knew what was happening, he had taken her hand to squeeze it politely but she was melding hers to it, the urge to heal those scars racing through her fingertips like a gust of hot air escaping from a vent.

She couldn't heal them—not scars—there was nothing to fix. She'd worked with scarred people to no avail. But the power reacted instinctively for those few seconds, until she willed it into obedience. She let go of his hand abruptly and curled her fingers shut.

"Kyle, are you all right?" asked his wife, Sara, a petite strawberry-blond with worry stamped on her elfin face. He rubbed his hands together and stared at them. "No more champagne for me. My fingers felt numb, or something."

Elena coughed. "We Russian women have strong grips. We would do well in arm wrestling, *dah*?"

The group's soft laughter was no antidote for the scowl on Audubon's face. When she met his eyes, he sent a private look of warning her way. She gave him a prim smile that said she would do as she pleased. His friends couldn't possibly guess what was happening when she touched them, and she would harmlessly create feelings of comfort and goodwill.

And wouldn't harm herself, if she didn't let her power get out of control.

After the introductions he took her to a group of sofas in front of the room's massive fireplace. On a warm spring night there was no need for a fire, and considering her mood, no need for more warmth. One of the men sat down at the baby-grand piano in a corner and began playing a soft classical piece. Everyone else sat down around her.

She clasped her hands in her lap and tried to sound relaxed as she answered their pleasant questions. They only knew that she was a secretary from Moscow; she could be vague about the rest. Audubon was a stern presence who leaned against the fireplace mantel with his arms crossed, watching her through hooded eyes. A fox watching his prey, she thought with anger. Did he think she would embarrass him?

One of the wives sat down in the armchair close to where she sat on the sofa and spoke to her in halting Russian. Tess Surprise, that was her name. She had a headache, but she was gallantly ignoring it. Elena couldn't. It was begging to be erased.

"How beautiful!" Elena said, and took her hand to admire a ring.

"It was a gift from my husband when our son was born last year. A blue diamond. I have a sentimental fondness for them, and . . ." Tess Surprise touched her forehead, frowned, then lifted her eyebrows and shrugged. Elena knew the headache was gone. "What was I saying?"

"It's a lovely ring," Elena coached.

"Oh, yes. Well, excuse me, I think I'll run upstairs and see if Clarice is having any problem being a baby-sitter." She left, looking thoughtful and confused. Her husband, Jeopard, followed her and shot Audubon a questioning look on the way out.

Elena knew people were growing more intrigued now. A giant, dark-haired man sat down in the chair Tess Surprise had just vacated. Everyone talked pleasantly again, and she tried to concentrate on discussing *perestroika* and *glasnost* and all the other trendy Russian-American issues, but her hand kept itching to grasp her next-door neighbor's.

Itching. He had some kind of itching problem, and as long as he sat this close to her, she would feel it on her own skin. When Bernard came by with a tray of glasses filled with champagne, the giant grabbed one and drank it in a gulp.

"Excuse me for drowning my sorrows," he said to everyone, chuckling grimly. "But I have the worst case of poison ivy in medical history. I chased my wife through the woods last week, and all I have to show for it is an urge to have my legs sandblasted from the knees down."

"That's not what you said at the time," Echo Lancaster commented. She winked at him, smoothed long black hair back with a cinnamon-skinned hand, and smiled at the group. "I was trying to make him feel at one with nature, like a Cherokee. Instead he only feels at one with a tube of cortisone cream."

Elena rested a hand on his tuxedo-clad arm, as if in sympathy. "You have this terrible 'poison ivy' all over you?"

"We'd better not be specific about where he has it," his wife interjected, grinning.

He tried to smile, but his eyes were riveted to Elena's hand. "But it was worth the—do you have a fever?"

She was done, thank goodness. With a sigh of relief she drew her hand into her lap and feigned surprise. "A fever? Are you making a joke?"

"I . . . no, never mind. Too much champagne. I need some air. Excuse me."

Looking bewildered, he rose and extended a hand to his wife, who strolled with him out to the prettily lighted pool.

"My champagne must be unusual tonight," Audubon noted from his guardian place by the mantel. "First Kyle comments on it, now Drake."

Elena ignored him. Someone else had taken Drake's place. One of the wives, and she had indigestion.

There were two dozen people here, and all of them had some little ache or pain that she could fix. She felt a little tired, but she would pace herself. The evening was going as she'd hoped, even though Audubon wasn't reacting the way she wanted. His mood worsened as she grew more comfortable and moved around the room, talking to people, touching them whenever she could find an excuse, winning their curiosity and smiles.

He remained a silent, dark force in the background, watching her constantly, his expression just short of being angry, or maybe hiding more anger than she realized. She didn't know what she was doing wrong, but she knew she couldn't stop. It began to scare her, because she could feel deep fatigue creeping through her body. But she *was* pacing herself, and as long as she did that, she would be fine.

As the hours passed, the laughter and conversation surrounded her like honey for a queen bee. Everyone felt wonderful, and several commented to Audubon that she had a way of making people relax, or forget their troubles, or *something*. She was a success.

A very tired success, now worried she wouldn't have the energy to climb the stairs when it came time to say good night. She slipped out of the room finally, intent on going to the enormous kitchen deep inside the manor and making herself a strong cup of coffee.

She walked slowly down a narrow side hallway that angled through the back of the house, her feet weighted, her chest heavy with exhaustion. It was a servant's route, with bare walls and linoleum floors, and she liked the simplicity. Her tormented feelings over Audubon cried out for this calm little place.

"Stop, please. I want to talk to you."

Audubon. She put a hand on the wall to steady herself, turned gracefully, and waited with a thready pulse as he approached her. His shoes made clipped, authoritative sounds on the linoleum; his head was up and his body wired with tension.

"Yes?"

"What the hell have you been trying to do tonight?"

He stopped less than an arm's length away, and his fury washed over her. There was pain in him, but not the kind she could heal with her touch. "I have been trying to make a good impression on your friends."

"I told you these men were off-limits."

As his meaning sank in, her lips parted in amazement. She leaned harder on the wall, and locked her knees to keep from swaying. "I was just as friendly to their wives as to them. How can you accuse me of . . . what are you accusing me of? Trying to steal them from their wives? Oh, Audubon." His name came out with a soft, bitter moan.

"Stop touching them. I don't care how innocent it seems. I know you don't have much experience in social settings, or with 'free' men, meaning men who haven't been instructed by Kriloff to keep you occupied, but—"

"But you don't think I have any morals, either!"

"That's not true. I merely believe you're eager to see how much influence you have now that the ugly duckling has become a swan."

"Are you blind?" Shivering with rage, she wanted to slap him. But hurting him was beyond her comprehension. "Are you blind?" she repeated softly, brokenly, and turned away, leaning her head against the wall. She laughed wearily. "Again, I'm some kind of bird to you. Right now I feel like one who's crashed. Leave me alone."

"I'll say your good nights for you. I think we've both accomplished what we intended for this party. Different goals, unfortunately. But it's over. Take the back staircase and go up to your suite."

He walked away without giving her a chance to answer, to tell him she was no child to be ordered to her room, that he was proud, stupid, and had no right to be jealous or judgmental. After he left she decided dignity wouldn't let her use the back stairs. She returned to the main hall, intending to head for the staircase in the front foyer.

"Elgiva, it's all right. Please, calm down."

"I'll get Douglas."

Elena halted, listening to the anxious female voices. They came from a sitting room tucked into an alcove at the other end of the hall. She went to it as quickly as she could, using the wall for balance. Sara, Kyle's wife, hurried out of the alcove and almost bumped into her. Elena took her arm. "What's wrong?"

"Elgiva may be having a miscarriage. I'm going to find Douglas."

In the alcove Tess sat on the floor next to a small couch, where Elgiva lay, her head propped on the armrest, her knees bent and bare feet braced against the opposite armrest. Her beautiful blue gown was a stark contrast against her ashen skin. Tears streaked her face. She had both hands on her abdomen.

"I started having terrible cramps a few minutes ago," she whispered, as Elena sank to the floor beside her. "And I'm bleeding a little. I'm going to lose the only bairn I've ever had—the only one Douglas and I might ever have, for all I know."

Elena felt as if her bones would turn to soft wax at any second. This was the last thing she ought to do, after such a tiring night. The other things had been nothing but parlor tricks, compared to this. She thought about the danger for the length of time it took her to gently push Elgiva's hands away and put hers in their place.


Audubon was in his study, brooding, a glass of cognac in hand, when Jeopard found him. They ran to the alcove, where Elena was unconscious on the floor. Tess Surprise held her head and Elgiva held one of her hands, while Douglas knelt beside Elgiva, an arm around her. One of the other wives, a physician, was checking Elena's pulse. The rest of the crowd waited quietly in the hall.

Audubon groaned under his breath when he saw Elena's face. It was nearly as pale as the ivory carpet. He sank down and took her hand from Elgiva. It was limp and cold.

"Her pulse is very weak," the physician said. "I think she should go to a hospital."

Audubon pulled her into his arms. Her head fell loosely, terrifying him. She was as fluid as a dream in his arms, and as difficult to hold. "Elena," he begged in a hoarse whisper. "Come back." He tucked her head against his shoulder and held her fiercely. "What happened?"

He listened in a daze as Elgiva explained. She choked on tears. All she knew was that she wasn't in pain anymore. Oh, God, he understood now. But why had it put Elena in this desperate state? She hadn't been like this after saving his life, and that couldn't have been easier.

Elgiva touched Elena reverently. "The last thing she said was, 'Your baby is fine now. I promise.' Audubon, what did she do?"

"She healed you. If she said the baby is fine, then you can believe her. She's a healer." He rocked her and couldn't keep his voice from breaking. "She's incredibly special."

There were soft gasps and murmurs from the people crowded around them; men who were shocked by nothing were asking each other and their wives questions about what they'd felt when Elena touched them. Audubon was so frightened that he heard their voices through a veil of shock; inside it were only he and Elena, and everything was quiet except for the barely perceptible sound of her breathing.

"Come back," he whispered into her ear, urgently. "This isn't freedom. Don't go alone. Come back. Stay with me."

"Her pulse is a little stronger," the physician noted. "But not good."

Audubon slid an arm under Elena's legs. "Someone call Mac to meet us at the helicopter. That will be faster."

But before he could pick her up, she murmured his name and moved a little. His heart racing, he grasped her chin and tilted her head back so he could study her. Her coppery lashes flickered, then lifted. Even the strange, faded blue that he'd seen before couldn't make her eyes any less glorious to him. She seemed barely able to hold her lids open, but she looked at him with recognition—and love. "I'm taking you to a hospital," he said gently.

Her lips moved just enough to let faint sounds through. "No . . . only rest. Nothing else . . . helps."

"Are you sure?" He stroked her face with his fingertips, trying to give back the mysterious force she had said everyone shared. "It will be safe. No one will find you. I swear."

"No good. Only . . . sleep."

"This has happened to her before?" the doctor asked.

"Yes, but not this severely."

"I still think she should be examined in a hospital."

"Audubon." Her voice was so weak that he had to put his ear close to her lips to hear it. "Don't want . . . strangers . . . testing me . . . anymore. Please."

"I'm not going to let anyone humiliate you. But I'm afraid that you need medical care."

"No. I swear. Sleep."

His chest was tight with fear, but the pleading look in her eyes tore him apart. "No hospital, then."

He carried her upstairs to his suite. Her breathing was more normal, but she remained slumped in his arms. In the soft light of a Tiffany lamp beside his bed, her skin looked rosier than before, but he wasn't sure if it was just the lamp's illusion. She sank into the silk sheets and large pillows with a grateful sigh.

Audubon sat beside her, holding her hand tightly and caressing her forehead with his fingertips. "This is what Kriloff meant. You could destroy yourself unless you're careful. And you know that. Why did you push the limits all night?"

Her face seemed small and fragile inside the frame of blond hair and ivory pillow. Blinking slowly, her eyelids threatening to stay shut each time, she still managed to look determined. "It's all I have to give. My value."

He bent his head and held her hand to his cheek. "No. It's only one part of what makes you special. You don't have to use it to be loved."

"Had to help Elgiva."

"But the others—no. They would have been drawn to you anyway."

"I wasn't . . . trying to draw the men . . . the way you thought."

Audubon shut his eyes and kissed her upturned palm. Her fingers feathered gently over his cheek. The terrible coldness was fading from them. "Forgive me," he whispered. "I didn't want to share you with them."

Her whimper was the sweetest note of an inner song. "I love you. No matter . . . what happens."

Stunned, he cleared his throat and said gruffly, "Nothing bad will happen. You're going to rest. I'll be right here, all night." *Forever.* "Try to sleep."

He reached beneath her and unfastened the top buttons of her bodice, pulled it down her shoulders, and stroked his spread hand along her neck. He wanted to draw her pulse to the surface of her skin, bring her strength back, promise her life. Her eyes opened a little wider, solemn and trusting. With his fingers resting just above her breasts he gauged her slowly moving chest, and every breath of his own was in sync with hers. He leaned down and kissed her. "Do you know? Can you tell? Have you been blind all this time, yourself?"

The blue of her eyes became more vivid as he watched. Small miracles were taking place every second. "Yes," she whispered. "But would you say it out loud for me?"

"I love you, Elena. I love you, dear dove. And no one is ever going to take you away from me."

She smiled and fell asleep. Audubon watched her with tears on his face. Promises were planted like flower seeds between them.

# *Eight*

She woke the next morning with his arm wrapped snugly around her waist, and the delicious angles and textures of his body only a wish away. Coming out of many hours of leaden sleep caused by her exhaustion, she let his nearness and the fresh day's anticipation soar through her blood, but she lay still, not turning her head to look at him yet, enjoying the moment with her eyes shut, recreating what she remembered.

*I love you, dear dove.*

During the night she'd awakened enough to know that he was removing her clothes down to nothing but her full-length white slip and panties. She remembered his hands on her thighs as he removed her garter belt and hose, then his fingers gently tugging her bra from under the slip. His touch had been sensual, but not sexual. He didn't linger or coax—there was nothing self-serving about his attention—but he imprinted his tenderness on her skin.

Then he'd kissed her forehead and gotten into bed beside her. Naked? Even now she didn't know. His body wasn't quite touching hers, except for his arm. Listening to him breathe was a small delight in itself. The great Audubon asleep! It hardly seemed possible the man indulged in something that made him so defenseless, so vulnerable to dreams and temptations. She loved him with a fierce ache in the center of her chest. The future would be wonderful. She was determined.

She made herself wait to look at him. Deliberately she trained her eyes on the white ceiling and its elaborate wood molding, then on the riot of sinfully plush pillows, tapestries, and upholstered chairs, which oddly enough produced a nestlike security. It made his bedroom the most peaceful den she could imagine. The outside world was muffled by the heavy drapes. She had awakened in a glorious cocoon, with the best companion in the world.

Slowly she turned her head to look at him. They shared a pillow; he was so close, she could count each dark brown eyelash and smile at the natural curl of the tips. His mouth was solemn, unfrivolous territory with a sensual lower lip that made exploration irresistable. Every sculpted angle and line of maturity proclaimed the vital, primitive sexuality of the male face.

Would everything be all right between them this morning? She hadn't imagined his words last night. She knew they'd torn down the most important barrier both he and she had built. But this was an enormous leap forward in hopes, in dreams.

Breathless, she turned on her side and closed the small distance between them, mewing softly when her body settled against his. The contact was even more affecting than she'd thought, and she began trembling inside, her senses threatening to dance over the edge.

Even still asleep he was aware of her explosive invitation. He shifted languidly, then his topmost leg curled over both of hers, his arm snaked farther around her waist, and to her delight she found herself captured inside a provocative, full-length embrace. Every tender emotion and fierce need met in an uncontrollable reaction; she arched against him and shuddered, biting her lip to keep from crying out in joy and astonishment. Her body writhed without really moving, held still by shock and willpower, but her restraint only sent the sweet ache deeper, where it pulsed.

She was dazed and panting when the sensations withdrew to a safe distance, but they lingered there without fading completely, a marvelous storm that could shift toward her again with the slightest change of currents.

The man was still asleep! She was pleasantly embarrassed by what had happened. He hadn't touched her, kissed her, or even looked at her, but here she lay in the afterglow of making love to him.

And wanting, already, to do it again.

Flushed, quivering, wide-eyed, she huddled against the restless little movements he began to make. He wore pajama bottoms. She smiled. He was such a gentleman. Her smile turned into a silent, ecstatic oh! when he swiftly became aroused inside their silk confines. Even asleep, he prodded her belly with lusty welcome. The *best* kind of gentleman.

He gave a long, slow, sigh of pleasure—such an enticing sound, half-exhalation, half-growl—that she shivered in happy response. Elena nuzzled the crook of his neck. The sumptuous, brocaded bedcover, silk sheets, and fluffy pillow contrasted and conspired with his hard, lean body. She felt the lovely turbulence gliding back.

Incredible. Disturbing. He was going to wake up in the midst of all this and think her strange, desperate, or at least self-centered. She was to the point where she didn't know if she cared about appearances as long as he wanted her immediately. Elena angled her face up to his and sank both a moan and a kiss onto his slightly parted lips.

Awareness rippled through him. Suddenly the heavy, quiet muscles flexed and woke. Suddenly his eyes opened and stared directly into hers. He lifted his head, dragged at her lips as he left them, and looked down at her in shock. "What's wrong? *Elena!*" He was on his knees instantly, pulling the covers back, staring anxiously at her, cupping her face in his hands. "You're burning up. *Make it stop.* Darling, you can control this. Concentrate. Don't let it hurt you."

"Nothing's wrong, Audubon." Dismayed, she stroked his shoulders. "Don't be afraid. I'm all right."

"Your face is so damned flushed." He ran his fingertips over the damp skin of her throat and chest. "You're breathing like a bellows and you're so damp that your slip is sticking to you. Dammit, listen to me. Turn it off. I love you. Why are you letting this thing take over? Fight it, for my sake, at least. You don't need to prove anything to me. No more exploding flowers. No more hot-wired psychic massages. They aren't necessary."

"Oh, Audubon, it's not what you think. Please, calm down. Come here. Please. I can barely make sense right now, but believe me, I'm perfectly all right."

He went very still, scrutinizing her. "Don't keep any more secrets from me, Elena."

She chuckled shakily. "Touch me, and you'll learn the truth."

"I *am* touching you, and it's practically burning my hands. I was a fool for not taking you to the hospital last night." He rubbed his hands over her bare shoulders, snagging the slip's thin straps in his hurried examination. She whimpered as the lacy bodice scrubbed her breasts. He grabbed her shoulders roughly. "Why didn't you tell me that you wouldn't be well by morning?"

She gave up on rational conversation. "There's only one way that you can make me feel better."

He crouched over her, ready. "What is it?"

Elena licked her lips nervously and tried to sound convincing. "The energy flow must be disrupted. You must use your energy to break the pattern. Put your hands on my sides."

Audubon clamped his hands to her waist. "Here?"

"Yes. Now, very slowly, slide them down my hips. Make certain that all of your fingers press firmly."

The delicious compliance of his hands made her

shut her eyes. Looking at him as he followed her instructions was too much temptation. She must stop this immediately and try to make him understand that she was suffering only from a sweet yearning for him. He was worried about her.

"Now what?" he asked. He gripped the outsides of her thighs.

"Audubon," she said with gentle rebuke, "there's really no need for all this concern."

"Either tell me what to do next, or I'm taking you to the hospital."

She'd tried to be honest, hadn't she? With gracious defeat she whispered, "Flatten your hands on my stomach and slide them upward to my chest."

His face set in serious lines, he did as she asked. She struggled not to make a sound. "Now back down the same path. Slowly. Yes. That's right. The energy is . . . following your hands. Distracted."

He stopped with his hands spread on her lower abdomen, the backs of his thumbs lightly resting against the feminine crest behind them. "What's happening to you?" he demanded grimly. "You've started quivering."

"It's just the effect of your hands on my energy patterns. It means you're doing exactly the right thing. Draw your fingertips down my thighs, please."

She felt the creamy slip pucker and tighten under his large, gentle fingers. She felt the indentation of every finger on her inner thighs. Rivulets of pleasure ran upward and converged inside her belly. "You're only feeling hotter to me," he said anxiously. "Love, please try to concentrate. I feel so damned helpless."

Elena looked at him tenderly. "Audubon, stop." The sublime passion mingled with increasing guilt. This wonderful, caring man was frightened for her, while she enjoyed herself at his expense.

"No, I'm not convinced that it's safe." He molded his hands to her stomach and rubbed small circles. "Maybe closer contact would accomplish more." He jerked the slip up to her thighs and put his hands underneath. Her protests dissolved in helpless gasps. "Elena, I'm being serious. Relax."

Relax? She was caught as before in spontaneous and overwhelming sensation. Dimly she realized she was calling his name, while she turned her face toward the pillow and let waves of release twist her body under his hands.

Audubon's surprise was followed by quick exploration of an intimate nature that would tell feminine secrets to any experienced male. When his hand slid under her panties, she moaned in soft, unbroken supplication.

He murmured a curse filled with relief and shock. Abruptly his exploration became a skilled caress, a little rough in rebuke, designed to taunt her with the pleasure he knew his touch provided. He caught her chin in one hand and made her look at him.

Elena was limp and trembling, unable to do anything but cling to the fierceness in his green eyes. There was also dark sensuality in them, as the situation sank in, but mostly anger. "I tried to tell you," she whispered. "More than once."

"I can't remember when anyone's manipulated me so blatantly. Me! The master of manipulation."

"Don't be hurt. That's the last thing I intended."

"I thought you were about to burn out like a candle. But *you* were getting your jollies. You hooked me like a trout."

"Jollies? Trout? Please, what are those?"

"Never mind. You smug little con artist." He was so close that his breath feathered her lips. He looked not too adverse to kissing them, but she couldn't be certain. He continued to stroke her with the same slow, forceful movements of his fingers. "Are you or are you not fully recovered from what happened last night?"

"I'm fully recovered. Sleep and rest are the only treatments. I swear to you, there's nothing for you to worry about now. I love you for your worry, but you must trust me. I don't intend to destroy myself when I help others. I don't take foolish chances."

"Elena, when I woke up and looked at you, your face was red and you were breathing as if you were having an asthma attack.'"

"Hasn't that happened to your women before? I thought you were a worldly man. A man who knows what he's seeing when he looks at a woman who finds him exciting."

"But you, dear Russkie, couldn't be any more unique if you tried. I spend half my time trying to get information from you and the other half wishing I could understand what I do get."

"I didn't mean to deceive you a few minutes ago. But I was embarrassed to tell you what had happened." She spoke very softly. "I don't know the correct words to describe this in English . . ."

"Try," he growled.

"I had just made love to myself, on your behalf."

She saw the explanation click in his mind. "Aaaah," he said, looking startled. Then the sensual droop to his eyelids showed he was thinking about the moment he'd awakened with her overheating in his arms, and also imagining what had occurred to put her in that state. He cupped his palm to her and drummed his fingers lightly on a very sensitive spot.

"You'll have to show me how you accomplished this interesting phenomenon. I can't decide quite what you mean, since you don't know the proper English description."

"I doubt there's anything *proper* between you and me at this moment." They were both speaking in a hushed, private tone made for intimacy. His hand began visiting other regions under her slip. The bedcovers tantalized her widely spread feet; each time she curled her toes, the brocade coverlet seemed to be kissing them.

"Please, Ms. Petrovic, *do* try to explain," he urged, as if a deep baritone voice could sound prim. "The Victorian setting demands propriety."

She couldn't match his teasing mood. What had happened to her was too special. Feeling tears pool in her eyes, she told him softly, "I woke up thinking about you last night, the way you cared for me, the way you touched me. I moved close to you. You held me. I would never have believed that a woman could feel so much just from a man's embrace. If I'm unique, then so are you, my love."

His eyes burned her with their pleasure and intentions. "Come here," he ordered. Playful talk was discarded for deep, erotic kisses and the shared melody of encouraging whispers and moans. She caressed him through his black pajama bottoms, smoothing the material over his legs and abdomen, fitting her hands into the hard angles and curves covered in fluid silk.

He caught his breath as the soft tie string gave up its duty to her nimble fingers, which were soon feathering over his naked belly, discovering everything about him. Velvety hot skin, coarse hair that tickled, and fascinating shapes transmitted waves of delight up her fingertips and back to him.

Audubon rolled over and dragged her across his chest, while one hand sank into the back of her slip. Already the hapless garment was barely covering her, the straps hanging down her arms, the bodice lace caught only on her nipples. Now his quick tug pooled it around her waist. He winked at her, so satisfied with himself, and she laughed, until his skillful hands and inventive mouth proved how right he was to be confident.

They undressed each other slowly. He lay on his stomach with his head and arms draped over one side of the bed while she nibbled and kissed him. She found herself sitting with her back braced against a bedpost, her hands wound tight around the carved wood behind her head, while he sat facing her, his feet tucked mischievously under her updrawn legs. The bedcovers jumbled around them in hummocks of fine fabric that tantalized by discreetly hiding, here and there, an attraction, an invitation, a blatant caress.

Sometimes she and he were polite, asking permission. *May I? Would you like it?* Then politeness would succumb to a selfishness that wasn't selfish at all, because it was designed to excite.

"We should stop now, before we go too far," he teased in a low voice raw with desire, as they faced each other, kneeling, fingertips tracing the differences and similarities between their bodies. "Go downstairs, have some breakfast—"

"What an ego! I've let you get away with it for too long!"

Seconds later they were tangled in the center of the bed, and his body pressed hers deeply into the delicious nest. She trembled as he stroked her hair, then cupped his hands under her head. His thumbs caressed the corners of her lips, then rubbed across the swollen surface to receive kisses.

He looked down at her with the flushed, tense expression of a man trying very hard to keep the necessary control. "Audubon," she said desperately, already beginning to ache inside.

"Don't let it happen," he ordered, his eyes alight with pleasure at what they both knew would occur when he entered her. "It will be too much for me."

But she whimpered with anticipation, and curled her legs around him tighter. "It's your fault."

His sloe-eyed scrutiny was an erotic challenge. "I take the blame. But only because I love you so much."

"I forgive you for making me this way."

"You might reconsider. I'm not done, yet. Not for hours, actually. And of course, we're not just talking about this morning. There'll be this afternoon, tonight, tomorrow—"

"Stop." A vibration ran through her at the wonderful images. "I accept my fate."

He settled deeper between her legs, teasing, moving forward. "Be calm. Use your willpower. I insist."

"Audubon, you dear monster. You *dear* tyrant. *Audubon*." As he sank deep inside her she cried out and arched repeatedly, clinging to him, while his own body shivered with control. She heard him saying wonderful words to her, praising her in lusty and gentle ways. But he lay still, every muscle braced, waiting for her to quiet a little. When she did, he began to move in a very slow cadence.

"Don't hold back," she urged, nuzzling his ear and kissing the damp, warm side of his neck. She was floating in another dimension, and she wanted him there with her. "I love you."

"I want this to go on forever."

She drew back and smiled at him. He stared at the love she felt shimmering in her eyes, then gave up *forever* with noble defeat. His sudden wildness made her wrap her arms around him and bury her head on his shoulder, crooning to him in Russian, loving the way his chest hair brushed her cheek in rhythm with his fierce movements.

He nuzzled her head back and kissed her, then kept his mouth lightly on hers, whispering her name. She felt the sensual twist of his body as pleasure shot through him. They were beyond perfection, balanced on the cusp of one of the greatest mysteries they could share.

Afterward, shaken and breathless, he met her eyes again. This time he smiled back, disheveled, vulnerable, completely open. "Wait here, darling."

He kissed her and lifted himself from her body, while she watched with bewilderment and rebellion, not wanting him to go. But he only stretched out on his stomach next to her, leaned over the edge of the bed, and pulled something from underneath. "Thank you," he said softly.

She turned over and craned her head alongside his. On the floor was a mountain of flowers blooming from a miniature white rosebush. Elena put her arms around Audubon's neck as he twisted to face her, studying her reaction intensely. "Were you testing me?" she asked.

"Testing myself, to see if I could make you happy."

She snuggled against his chest and held him tightly. "I could fill this room with flowers."

"You've already filled it with miracles."

She managed to catch her breath enough to kiss

him. Then they curled up in each other's arms and began making the miracle, again.


Elena was never far from his thoughts, even now. How could he put aside the memories of the long, glorious day they'd spent together? His offices had a secluded atmosphere that he ordinarily found appealing—the solitude had been part of him for years, and the unchanging artificial light in the windowless rooms made time seem endless . . . and forgiving.

But it wasn't. It demanded decisions and action. Dressed in rumpled trousers and a long silk robe of oriental design, Audubon went from fax machine to telephone messages from his people in Mexico. An old enemy's hatred struck out at Audubon.

*A son for a son,* Miguel de Valdivia warned.

At dawn, several hours after the phone in his suite buzzed with Clarice's call, Audubon dragged himself upstairs. He found Elena asleep on a couch in his study. The glow of a lamp gave her blond hair a warm, feminine contrast to the burnished leather, and her hands were furled gently against the collar of a white turkish robe.

She had dressed for propriety, he thought with a pang of affection, noting the bulky robe and the high neckline of a blue satin nightgown. Looking at her, no one would suspect that nakedness suited her the way it suited a Greek statue, that earlier that day she had danced for him wearing nothing but a lace curtain draped around her, that she'd fed him grapes while he played the violin in bed. Both of them had been laughing, naked, as joyful as children.

Her carefree moments were just for him. He knelt beside her and smoothed a hand over her head.

"Audubon." She rubbed her eyes and sat up quickly. "I was worried when you stayed away so long."

"I'm sorry, love." He was surprised by feelings of guilt for not bringing her down to the offices. Years ago he'd accepted the need for secrecy, and no lover had ever been part of his work.

"Is the emergency finished?"

"For now." It was brewing, not finished, but there wasn't anything else he could do that night. He sat down on the floor and leaned back against the couch, massaging his forehead wearily. "You must have a thousand questions."

"And you don't want to answer any of them." She spoke without rebuke. "I don't think it's because you distrust me, so I'm not hurt. Not too much, anyway."

He chuckled. "You know more about me than anyone else in the world. Be patient."

"You know me too."

"I know that you love ballet, peanut butter, and *borscht*; that when you were growing up, you watched Elvis movies dubbed in Russian; that you want to hike the Grand Canyon and visit Disney World; that you favor simple clothes and complex books. A hundred little things. That leaves slightly less than a million more to learn."

"Give me time. I've been preoccupied." She caressed his cheek and looked at him somberly. "Is your adopted son still in trouble?"

"Yes."

"Will you be going back to Mexico?"

"Perhaps. The next few days will tell." He leaned his head against the couch, and she rubbed his temples. He felt the tingling glow in her fingertips. She was relaxing him, making the dull tension fade, seducing him so he'd confide in her.

And possibly say too much. She must never know she'd been a game piece in his plans. It would destroy everything between them. He'd spent the past few hours plotting his new course of action—and its consequences made sharp pain well in his chest.

"What's wrong?" she whispered, and laid her cheek against his hair. "What hurts you so much?"

"Turn off your psychic antennae. You're getting your signals crossed. I have a headache, that's all." He reached behind him and grasped her hands then pulled them in front of him, where he gently trapped them inside his own. "There. Behave, my little Slavic nymph."

"I'm too old and large to be a nymph. And too modern. Yes. I'm going to be a sophisticated American woman, like the ones in all your magazines."

"So you're going to consult your horoscope, try a new diet every week, learn how to power-walk, power-dress, and have power-lunches, while doing a study of techniques for keeping your boss, lover, husband, parents and/or children free of waxy buildup. Oops. Pardon me. I'm getting my articles confused."

"You're very smug." But her tone had a smile in it. "No, I'm just not going to be passive and dependent."

"You're neither of those now."

"Oh? I have no money and no home, and I depend on you for everything."

"And that bothers you?"

"Am I your mistress? Is that what Americans call it?"

"No, you're my personal love slave. How's that?"

"Hmmmph. It requires one to know one."

"It *takes* one to know one. Yes, you're right. We're in the same boat as love slaves."

"What's this about boats?"

"Never mind." He rubbed his thumbs across the backs of her hands, doing a little seducing of his own. "So you don't want to depend on me."

"I don't want you to feel sorry for me. I'm not one of your rescue missions. I'm not a child you can adopt. Where do I fit into your life?"

"I don't think there's any point in discussing this until you're established in this country as a permanent citizen. How can you know what you want until then?"

"I want a bookstore. With a coffee machine and comfortable chairs and lamps in one corner, and a stereo that plays pleasant music to read by. I want my own home to come back to every night with a cat that purrs when it sees me and a dog that wags its tail."

"I've always planned to invest in a bookstore. And

I think I'd like to have a dog. I had a dog once, when I was little. A champion Afghan. I got to pet it every morning when the trainer took it for a walk. Yes, a dog would be nice, as long as you didn't want a trainer with it. Cats don't impress me one way or the other—my mother had a Persian. Lady Alison of Gallantree, and she was only entertaining because she'd upchuck fur balls on the maid's bed."

"And how did you know what the cat did on the maid's bed?"

"I had an interest in housework, I was fourteen at the time. Housework fascinated me."

"She taught you a great deal about it, did she?"

"Fur balls?"

"Beds."

"She was plump and cuddly."

"The maid?"

"No, the cat."

Elena lowered her head beside his and bit his ear. "You love to manipulate a conversation, don't you?"

"Ouch. Yes. So . . . a bookstore, a dog, a cat, and a home. No problem. You can certainly consider this your home. I'm awfully glad we settled all that. I'm getting sleepy."

"Audubon, why haven't you married?"

Silence settled between them. He wanted the strained yet teasing mood to continue, but it had fallen like a soufflé. He wanted to tell her he had never considered marriage a worthwhile institution before he met her. But that discussion would have to wait until Kash's problem was settled. He wouldn't make promises he might not be alive to keep. And she might not want them anyway. "Not everyone is qualified to be married. In fact, damned few people are any good at it."

"Then all this talk about pets and bookstores is not a marriage proposal?"

"No. But it's an offer of genuine love and my way of telling you that I don't want you to leave me."

"I see. I'll have to think about it. So much has

happened to me in the last few weeks. My whole life has changed."

"And you're not certain if anything you feel right now is going to last."

"I didn't say 'I love you,' because I was confused. And I didn't mean that I love you *if* you marry me, or give me a bookstore."

"It's the dog and cat you're negotiating for, then," he joked weakly.

Her hands cooled. She pulled them away and got up from the couch. Audubon felt the whole conversation had gone badly, but for now he could only let explanations lay dormant. She scrutinized his face while frowning sadly. "I want to come out of hiding. It's time I went to your State Department and asked for asylum."

"Soon, but not now."

"Why are we waiting?"

"It's not safe yet. Be patient."

"You have reasons you won't admit."

"I want to protect you. More than ever." He got up, the silk oriental robe riding his shoulders like a mantle of lead. He felt a hundred years old. He felt cruel for keeping secrets from her. He knew he couldn't use her future to save his son's, so the only future he had left to bargain with was his own. He wanted all of her memories of him to be wonderful.

"I would rather die than let anything bad happen to you," he whispered. "Don't ever doubt that."

She grasped the front of his robe and stared up at him with fear in her eyes. "Don't say such things! Why do you have to be so melodramatic? You belong in a dark play by Chekhov!"

In a quick, powerful sequence of moves that caught her off guard, he swung her sideways, bent, scooped his arms under her, and picked her up. "I love you and I only want the best for you," he told her. "Men aren't nearly as good with words as women are, so all I can do is show you."

He carried her upstairs, but not to his suite. Instead he went to hers, and stopped outside. His throat was raw; his eyes had a grainy feel. Lack of sleep. Not emotion. He wouldn't let himself cry from worry and frustration, or even desperate love. He never had before and he was too old to start now.

"I don't make ugly demands on the people I love. You need time to realize that. Do you want to stay in your own room for now?"

"Yes."

He put her down and she went inside immediately, one hand cupped over her mouth as if she were about to cry. He went back to his own suite, almost stumbling with fatigue, loneliness throbbing painfully in his head. He was trapped in a lifetime of solitude, and he wondered if he'd found Elena too late. He had asked her to accept too much on faith.

Dawn made pale borders around the heavy drapes in his bedroom, giving the room a gray, cool light that seemed like emptiness incarnate. Audubon sat on the side of the bed, avoiding the moment when he'd have to lay down in the happily jumbled covers scented with crushed flower petals and passion. He rubbed his face harshly and tried to will his emotions back into the tidy vault inside him where they belonged.

From the front room came the soft rattle of the door latch. He walked in just as Elena slowly shut the doors behind her. She grew still and looked at him with faltering dignity that reminded him of his own. "How could such a lovely day turn into such a mess?" she whispered.

"Too much emotion floating around, I suppose. Some of it was bound to get misdirected."

"In America, is it common for two people who love each other to run off to separate bedrooms when they're upset?"

"I can only tell you that it was common for my parents." *But they didn't love each other.*

"They had too many bedrooms then."

He nodded. *Lord, am I blindly repeating their worst mistakes?* "I didn't want you to go. But I'm asking you to put aside too many questions. You can't really trust me right now. I understand."

"Trust, my love, is something I don't give and take back easily. I may be angry with you sometimes, but I believe in your goodness. I've felt it inside me, I've heard it in your voice, watched it in your actions, seen it in your eyes."

He couldn't answer. He simply held out a hand. She came over quickly and wrapped it in loving warmth. They walked to the bedroom and undressed in silence. She helped him smooth the covers and straighten the pillows. She got into bed first and pulled the covers up, then held them open for him to slide in beside her.

He put his head on her shoulder and sighed when she gently stroked his hair and face. When she touched his damp cheek, she smoothed the moisture into her fingertips as if his tears were the most precious gift he could offer.

# Nine

The clink of fine silver and the scent of sweet, warm bread woke her, and just as her eyes opened she realized she had slept with none of the restlessness she'd known all her life. The emotional confrontation before dawn seemed like a shadow that had faded with the night. It might return later, but she pushed it out of her mind for now. Her body felt pleasantly heavy, as if the muscles were soaked with relaxation.

"Good afternoon," Audubon whispered, kissing the tip of her nose. He was sitting beside her, one updrawn leg pressed cozily against her hip. She glanced down, wishing the covers and his crisp tan trousers didn't separate his skin from hers.

With the trousers he wore a white polo shirt with a tiny gold griffin stitched on the left breast. The shirt was custom-made, she knew, because he'd explained that all his clothes were created for him by an exclusive men's shop in England. The griffin came from the Audubon family crest.

A belt of fine, woven leather with a slender gold buckle circled his waist. His silver hair was glossy with brushing, every strand in its regal place. His hand, as he stroked his fingers down her cheek, carried the faint trace of some expensive cologne and a sweet citrus fragrance.

She decided not to comment on the purple shadows under his eyes, or the emotional distress etched in his face. She was worried about him and their situation, but she felt that talking about it might only make them both feel worse. She let herself float in his affectionate gaze. "You, sir, are a feast for my senses. But why are you fully dressed and out of bed, while I'm naked and most definitely *in* bed, waiting?"

His soft chuckle added to the sensual provocation. "I have a meeting downstairs in five minutes. I brought you breakfast."

She glanced at the silver teapot and china cup on the nightstand. Also on the small silver tray was a bowl of strawberries and cream, plus a plate filled with muffins covered in orange marmalade.

Elena took his orange-spiced fingers and kissed them. "I've never had breakfast in bed before. It's a very decadent American custom. Let's do it often."

"I look forward to it."

She reached over and ran a finger through the marmalade, then dabbed it to the center of his lips. He licked her fingertip, and his green eyes turned dark with intensity. But he clasped her willful hand and shook his head. "If I gave into temptation, I'd be here for hours."

"I'm afraid so. I'd tie you to a bedpost."

"I'd let you."

"Perhaps I'd just tie you to me."

"I'd let you."

She sighed. "Go to your meeting before I wrap my arms around your knees and refuse to let go."

"Now *that* could be interesting." He groaned in exasperation. "I wish I hadn't overslept, but it's your fault."

"I was minding my own business."

"You were breathing against my ear. I kept dreaming we were at the ocean. You were part of the tide. It was seductive, all that coming in and going out."

"I'd love to indulge your dream. I want to go back to the ocean. I'd never seen one before I came to

America. Looking at it made me feel there were no boundaries in the world."

"We'll go, then. I'll take you to beaches so beautiful, you can't imagine them."

"I'd love it." She cupped her hand along his face, caressing his cheek. "You really have to go downstairs this minute?"

"Afraid so. It's important."

She fought off the feeling of dull dread in her stomach. "The meeting's about your son?"

"Yes. Some of the men you met the other night are here to discuss his problem. This is one time when I'm asking for their help as friends, not former employees."

She hesitated, wondering if he were any less reluctant to trust her with his work. Elena had avoided asking questions because not asking was easier than being hurt by his secrecy. "Ask," he coaxed, reading her face with disturbing ease. "It's all right."

"What sort of work is Kash doing in Mexico?"

"He went to find the wife and children of an archaeologist who died recently."

"Forgive me—what is an archaeologist?"

"A scientist who studies the things left behind by ancient civilizations."

"Ah. You knew this scientist personally?"

"Yes. Dr. Juarez and I met in college. We'd been friends for more than twenty years."

"Oh, Audubon, I'm sorry he died. How did it happen?"

"He was shot while working alone at a project site. Murdered. He'd learned that a wealthy businessman was looting the ancient art treasures for a private collection. He was about to go to the police."

"You sent Kash to help his family?"

"Yes, to make certain they got out of the country. Kash accomplished that easily, but then he couldn't resist investigating the murder." Audubon smiled sadly, but with fierce pride glinting in his eyes. "I'm afraid I encouraged him to be too independent. He was supposed to leave the investigation to me. He didn't." Audubon drew a finger down one of her breasts and gently stroked the nipple. His distracted expression told her his thoughts were in Mexico, with his adopted son. His touch seemed to seek solace in her softness and warmth.

"He wanted to protect you?" she asked gently, thinking that Kash Santelli probably loved his adopted father very much, and with good reason.

"Yes. The businessman involved has a nasty reputation for revenge."

"Why would he want revenge against you?"

"I helped to destroy his son."

Her hands rose to her face in shock. "You mean his son died because of you?"

Audubon nodded. "Indirectly. He committed suicide rather than be exposed for what he was—a kidnapper and a spy. Remember Sara Surprise? Kyle's wife?"

The pretty elf with the strawberry-blond hair. Her husband, with his terrible scars. "Yes."

"She was one of the people he had kidnapped. That was before she met Kyle. She's a biologist. A researcher. Later I'll explain why she was kidnapped, but I don't have time now." He paused, grimacing. "The man who kidnapped her was responsible for Kyle's scars."

"And he was a spy on top of all that? Who did he work for?"

Audubon stroked her arm. "The Soviets."

Elena's horror made her turn away, pressing her fingertips over her mouth. Tears burned her eyes. "I see why you never wanted to discuss all this with me before. Is his father—the man who threatens Kash, now—is he a Soviet spy too?"

"Miguel de Valdivia? No, darling, he's just your garden-variety greedy bastard. Elena, come here." He pulled her into his arms and stroked her bare back. "There are plenty of self-serving, despicable people in the world. Your country has no monopoly on them. Don't take it personally."

"I'll feel dirty by association if that man does something terrible to Kash."

"Don't even *think* like that. This vendetta isn't about government intrigues; it's about fathers and sons. Kash has disappeared in Mexico. I don't doubt he's capable of taking care of himself, and I've sent some of my best people there to help him. He may just be in hiding. I'm still trying to find out."

She drew back and looked at him miserably. "I'm afraid for you."

"My dear dove, this crafty old fox has survived the hunt too many times to be outsmarted now." But then he kissed her deeply, pouring much more emotion into it than he had put into his words.

Breathing roughly, wanting to cry but adamant that she wouldn't, Elena tilted her forehead against his and shut her eyes. "When Kash is safely home, you'll have to introduce us."

"Of course. But he won't believe it, you know."

"Believe what?"

"That you beat me at checkers. I'll tell him you cheated."

"Oh, you!" She gave a hollow imitation of a laugh and shooed him off the bed. He walked to the bedroom door and paused, looking back with a sad, yearning expression that stabbed her.

"A wonderful new life is ahead of you," he said. "I hope it makes up for all those years at the institute."

She nodded, forcing herself not to admit what she was screaming inside: *Don't talk as if I'll be going on without you.*

She floated in his arms. Above them, the glass roof of the pool house showed a universe of stars. The night sky came right down through the glass and hovered around them, seeming to be careful not to creep too close to the cluster of candles by the pool's edge. The water reflected blue light and made the pool into a fantasy daytime sky. She felt protected by the shimmering light. Infinite amounts of time were locked in the light, the warm water, and Audubon's touch.

He cradled her in water so deep that when she leaned her head on his shoulder, the water lapped against her chin. She put her arms around his neck and turned her face toward the crook of his neck, then kissed the hollow of taut muscle just above his collarbone. For a moment she looked beyond the edge of the pool, where all of their clothes were jumbled together on a wicker chaise longue. "You're certain that Bernard won't be coming by to ask if we'd like after-dinner coffee, or anything else?"

"Bernard, my dear dove, has been politely instructed to scram for the night."

"Scram?"

"Vamoose. Take a powder. Beat it. Go away."

"I hope he doesn't bruise himself."

She felt the pull of Audubon's smile against her temple. "He's in his apartment."

"Oh. Very good."

"He and Clarice are probably playing footsie by now."

"What kind of game is that?"

"Well, in the case of Bernard and Clarice, I imagine that it involves one set of very dignified toes and one set of very naughty ones."

"Are you saying they're lovers?"

"Yes, they have been for several years. You'd never know it by watching them together during the day, would you?"

"No! They're extremely formal with each other."

"I walked into the library once and saw Clarice tickling him."

"What was Bernard doing?"

"Saying in his most solemn British-butler accent, 'Really, now, you she-beast, really.' But he was grinning. Not smiling. Grinning. I wanted to take a picture so I could show it to the rest of the staff, as proof that he has teeth."

Elena chuckled. "You adore both him and Clarice."

"Yes. I wish I'd had grandparents like them."

She smoothed a finger down his throat and into the silky, matted hair of his chest. Ah, she thought, his family mysteries. Trying to sound casual, she asked, "What were your grandparents like?"

"My father's parents didn't enjoy children, so whenever they visited I was shuttled off to another part of the house. I only remember their cheeks and their checks."

"What?"

"I dutifully kissed their cheeks each time the nanny presented me for inspection, and I received checks from them on my birthday and at Christmas. As for my mother's parents, they lived in Europe. I rarely saw them. To sum it all up, I wouldn't have cared if I'd had no grandparents."

"Oh, you would have cared. If you'd never met them, you'd always wonder what they were like. I'd give anything to have known mine."

*"Elena."* His voice was full of apology. "I'm sorry. I didn't think."

"Shhh. I stopped feeling sorry for myself years ago. When you grow up being alone, it eventually feels normal to you. You hear other people talk about their families and you think, 'How odd to have so many people care what happens to you!'"

Audubon rubbed circles in the small of her back. "I know. I've always wondered how people can see themselves as part of a group, instead of alone."

"I envy them."

"But I wonder if they feel suffocated sometimes."

"No, I suspect they feel cushioned. Without a family, there's no one around to catch you when you fall."

"Or to notice and remind you of your clumsiness."

"You certainly don't seem to mind having a son. What an interesting contrast to your cynical view of family life."

"Kash was already eight years old when Douglas Kincaid and I smuggled him out of Vietnam. And he'd lived a very rough life. It was like moving another adult into the house, not a little boy. Kash and

I have never been pals or confidants, the way fathers and sons are supposed to be."

Elena thought, *But your love for him shows every time you mention his name.* "Was *your* father your friend?"

"Hardly. I have better taste."

"Audubon, what happened to your parents and sister? And why did you sell the estate that had been in your family for generations?"

He was silent, and she lifted her head to look at him. "How did this conversation come to such a morbid subject? I will tell you sometime. But please, let's save tonight."

How bad could the story be? Elena's sympathy mingled with a dark urge to find out. He studied her face. "Don't be angry. If I didn't care so much about your opinion of me, it would be easier to share this. But I don't want to spend tonight discussing something so ugly."

The quiet anguish in him overwhelmed her questions. She kissed him. Changing the subject abruptly, she held up one wrist and nodded toward the small, oval bump beside the tendon. "When I come out of hiding, one of the first things I'd like to do is have this removed. From now on I want to make my own decisions about my body."

"Do you want children?"

"Someday, yes. For now I'd just like to know that I control the decision *not* to have them."

He circled her wrist with his fingers and rubbed the implant, as he studied it grimly. "I don't have any right to ask this, but . . ."

"How many men were there?" She gave him a victorious look. "I can read your thoughts."

"Hmmm. A psychic talent you haven't mentioned?"

"No, pure feminine intuition. But I have to remind you that I've never asked you about the women in your past. I was afraid I'd be shocked. I was certain I'd be jealous."

"Let's put it this way—there are too many for a string quartet but far too few to make a full orchestra. Not a large number considering how many years I've been a music fancier. Actually, I'd like to specialize from now on. I'm a one-instrument man, at heart."

She relaxed, patting his chest. "And you play it so well."

"Thank you." The lighthearted conversation didn't make him forget his earlier question. Winding his fingers through hers reassuringly, he said, "I'm only asking you about the past because this gut-wrenching fear won't leave me alone."

"Fear?"

"That you were treated like a clinical sex toy by dozens of men. I want to know how you feel about sex so I won't upset you in some unknown way when we make love. And frankly, I'd like to be certain that, after everything you went through, you can still enjoy the *romance* of it. I want you to very much."

"Dear man." Unable to say more without crying, she nuzzled his face lovingly until she could calm her voice. "I'll have to begin writing poetry for you as well as making flowers bloom. I doubt that my poems would be very eloquent, but they'd certainly come from the heart."

Tilting her head back, she held his gaze firmly and told him about the boy she'd known when she was twenty-one, and then about Pavel, who'd seemed so romantic and sincere but who'd only been following Kriloff's instructions to keep her occupied, while he reported on her progress.

Audubon looked relieved and sympathetic. "You should have had a few more men, so you'd know exactly how fantastic I am by comparison."

That broke the somber mood, and she was able to smile. "I have no doubt I've found the best. How many men could eat tangerines in bed without getting juice on anything except the breasts of the person next to them?"

"Why, I like fresh-squeezed juice and fresh-squeezed . . ."

"And how many men could recite Shakespeare while kissing delicate parts of the female body?"

"Not many. Especially when you kept interrupting with your pleas for more. It nearly ruined my concentration."

"I was asking for more Shakespeare, of course."

"Of course. Yes, I'm in a class by myself."

"And so humble about it."

"But let's keep talking about *you*. What do you like best about me?"

They broke into soft laughter at the same time. "Your good taste in choosing women."

Humming under his breath, he carried her to the side of the pool and lifted her up. The rough-grained stone edge gently abraded the backs of her thighs as she caught her balance. Then his shoulders were spreading her legs, and his hands were sliding up their inner surface, followed by his kisses.

His intentions were as clear as the night sky, and suddenly her skin was alive to its own universe of sensation. Audubon's arms slid under her legs, and his hands gripped the sides of her hips, helping her to lie back on the smooth tile floor. The pool sipped at her dangling feet. Droplets of water licked her belly as they trickled downward. Audubon began to trace the water's journey with his mouth. "You taste very good, indeed," he whispered.

Paradise was this night, and loving him.


The shrill chime of the telephone ended the waiting. Audubon grasped the portable unit from his nightstand before the first chime finished. He'd been awake for hours waiting for this, watching Elena sleep, stroking her hair.

Either she'd been pretending to sleep or sleeping lightly, because now she sat up and trailed a hand over his shoulders as he left the bed. He went to the room's large window and opened the drapes a few inches as he listened to the voice at the other end of the line.

A white quarter moon sat low in the sky. Its edges were so crisp that the moon looked like a crescent stamped out by a cookie cutter. That whimsical thought was a soothing contrast to the adrenaline pumping into his bloodstream. He told the caller he'd be leaving immediately, then cut the connection, and called downstairs to get the helicopter ready for a trip to the airport where he kept a small, private jet.

When he finally laid the phone down, Elena switched on the Tiffany lamp beside the bed. Her face looked serene in the soft light, but her blue eyes showed stark anxiety. "You're going to Mexico?"

"Yes, love. I have to."

She got to her knees on the edge of the bed and held out her arms. His emotions under guard, he stood stiffly beside the bed while she hugged him, with her head against the center of his chest. She sent her strange, wonderful glow through him, and he trembled.

God, he'd try his best to come back to her. If he didn't, arrangements had been made to transfer an enormous sum of money and valuable stocks to her. Jeopard, Kyle, and Drake would make certain Kriloff could never take her back to Russia. They'd help her settle in this country and see she got her beloved bookstore, her pets, her home.

She'd marry eventually, have children, and think about him less and less as the years passed. She'd keep her amazing gift a secret except to the trusted few she could help without destroying herself.

He wanted that version of the future for her, if he didn't come back, but right now the thought of it made him feel as though his heart were being ripped out.

She pressed her lips to a spot over his heart, then slid down, placing small kisses on his torso, then his sex, before rising again and lifting her face to his. "I'll be waiting, my handsome silver fox. I wish you could take my love and my powers with you to keep you safe."

"I take your love." He sank his mouth onto hers, tried to make it a kiss she'd never forget, and fought the ache in his throat.

"I'll keep yours," she whispered, tears sliding down her cheeks. "When you come back, we'll share."

"When I come back, I'll tell you my full name. That promise is our good-luck charm, all right? What a silly promise, but then, so is all this melodrama. I've tackled much more dangerous situations than the one down in Mexico."

She wiped her tears away and nodded brusquely. "Of course. We Russians are so morbid. It comes from reading *Doctor Zhivago* too many times when we're children. Something like that."

"Oh, I see."

They kept up the light banter while he showered and dressed. She sat on the side of the bed wearing his oriental robe. While chatting calmly, she wound its black silk belt around her fingers. He unwrapped her fingers and knotted the belt around her waist with a flourish. "You were pulling at it so hard, your fingertips had turned white," he said gently. "I was afraid your electromagnetic energy would back up and explode. How terrible. You might have a blow-out in your elbow."

"Oh, my. A flat elbow."

Her face was drawn with restraint. She smiled, but a blue vein showed in the translucent skin near one corner of her mouth. He couldn't talk to her any longer without admitting his misery, so he gritted his teeth and got ready to leave as quickly as he could. Drawing a long, lightweight white coat over his white trousers and open-necked white shirt, he paused for her inspection.

"I look like a fashionable Mexican businessman, I'd say. Either that, or I need a pair of goggles and a crank for my Model T."

Her blank reaction said that the very American joke was lost on her, but her admiration was clear nonetheless. She came to him and took his hands. "You make such a dramatic figure that everyone will be intimidated and do exactly as you say. You'll be back home by tomorrow. With Kash."

"No doubt at all." He framed her face with his hands, kissed her lightly on the mouth, then twisted away and grabbed a small leather suitcase he'd packed days ago in case of this emergency. With wooden efficiency he strode into the front room. She hurried after him, and he was afraid she'd cry and make the good-bye even more torturous. *I will see her again. I will come back.* Or die trying. He opened one of the suite's outer doors, winked at her, and stepped out quickly.

"Audubon, wait."

He bit back a groan as she glided into the hall, as graceful as a butterfly in his brilliantly colored robe, her bare feet making no sound on the thick tapestry carpet. She ran to a table and selected a jonquil from a vase there. She brought the unopened flower to him, gave him a jaunty thumbs-up, and held the jonquil out. It bloomed as he watched.

"Dear man, this is love." Smiling, she placed the flower in his outstretched hand then fled back into the suite, her cheerfulness crumbling. After he heard the doors shut, he exhaled a long, shaken breath. She was worth a lifetime.

# *Ten*

Even though Audubon had been gone less than two days, the mansion felt deserted and lifeless, like a castle with no king. But what alarmed Elena was Clarice and Bernard's somber mood. She watched them stare listlessly out the windows, their duties forgotten. Elena wandered from room to room, pretending to read a book in the library, talking to the chef about Russian recipes, trying to hide the fact that every nerve was tuned to a high pitch.

Her control evaporated when she walked into the great room and caught Clarice crying inside Bernard's distraught embrace. They pulled apart quickly. "I shouldn't watch soap operas," Clarice said, dabbing at her eyes. "I haven't cried this much since Nicki had an unknown fatal illness and tried to give Victor back to Ashley on *The Young and the Restless*."

"Tell me why you're so upset about Audubon," Elena begged, going to them with outstretched hands. "I'll lose my mind imagining the truth, if you don't. This couldn't be how you react every time he goes away on a job."

Bernard cleared his throat and looked at her kindly. "I assure you, we have no doubt that he and Kash will be fine. Audubon's work has never been without risks. You mustn't overreact. He'll be dismayed when he learns you're so frantic."

"Then tell me why the two of you are upset."

"Clarice and I are growing old. For us, worrying is a hobby. We prefer it to shuffleboard."

"Bernie, we can't do this to Elena," Clarice said hoarsely. "It's not fair."

"But it's what Audubon wants."

"He loves Elena, and she loves him. Hiding the truth from her right now is an insult to their love."

After a long moment in which Elena met Bernard's gaze with pleading silence, he sighed and nodded. "Yes."

Elena took his hands. "Tell me."

"Miguel de Valdivia is holding Kash at his ranch. Audubon has gone to trade himself for Kash."

"But that man hates Audubon! He might even kill—" She stepped back, ice-cold hands rising to her mouth in horror. "*Kill him.*"

"Yes," Clarice said, her voice breaking. "If the others can't find a way to get him out, he'll probably . . . die."

"The others?"

"The best people Audubon has working for him. Plus several of the old group—Jeopard and Kyle Surprise, Drake Lancaster. Also Douglas Kincaid is pulling some very powerful political strings to get help from the military. But Miguel de Valdivia is an important man in his country." Clarice sneered, as if she wished to spit something vile from her mouth. "The damned diplomats don't want an international incident."

Elena heard herself make an inhuman sound, a wail of grief merging with sheer rage. "I'm sick of diplomats and political maneuvers! I won't give Audubon to their insanity! I won't let them destroy him!"

She scarcely heard the chime of the manor's alarm system. Clarice grabbed her by the arm as Bernard ran to an intercom on one cherry-paneled wall. "What is it, Stephen?"

"Unusual visitors just crashed the party. When the Chief's away, the mice will play. Take cover."

"Another visit from the FBI," Clarice muttered. "Come on, Elena."

They ran to Audubon's study. Elena's white leather flats slipped on the carpet and she slammed one knee into a door facing. The pain made her head swim, but she ignored it. She had never been able to heal herself, but no pain could compete with her anguish over Audubon.

On their way to the inner office and its hidden door, Elena grabbed a small paperweight from his desk, desperate to have something that Audubon had touched. Her fingers vibrated against the smooth brown wood of a whimsically carved turtle. It was such an ordinary item that it must mean a great deal to him, she thought. *Audubon, feel me loving you. Feel me protecting you.* She shoved the funny little turtle into the pocket of her white shirtwaist dress.

A few seconds later she and Clarice were safely hidden in the underground rooms. The phone console beeped on Clarice's desk. She punched a button.

"They may stay here for hours," Bernard said in a low voice. "I won't be able to call you again."

Elena bent over the intercom. "Is Kriloff with them?"

"No."

Clarice was all business and fight. "I'll get on the private horn. See if I can jerk some tails and get these mice out of our hair." Her face softened for an instant. "You give 'em hell, Bernie."

"I'll freeze them to death with my good manners."

Elena paced the floor outside Audubon's office while Clarice phoned people whom she obviously knew well. She called them by their first names and, when they weren't forthcoming with help, by less polite names. Suddenly one of the fax machines began whirring. As Elena headed toward it, Clarice blocked her way. "The agents use those to send messages."

"About Audubon."

"About a lot of things. Let me decide if there's

anything you ought to know. Please, honey. I'm trying to take care of you."

"If Audubon is dead, I have to know." She pushed past Clarice and ran to the machine. It birthed a sheet of paper with maddening slowness, and she felt as if her muscles were being stretched on a rack.

Finally a dark, scrawled message emerged. *Cash and Carry. The Chief is on deposit. Going back for seconds when we get the contract.* It was signed. *The Iceman.*

A cry of frustration tore from Elena. "Speak English!"

Clarice put an arm around her shoulders. "Kash has been released," she translated. "Audubon has taken his place."

"Oh, dear God."

"But Jeopard Surprise and the others will try to help him. They're deciding the best way to go about it."

"But maybe there's no time."

"No, Miguel de Valdivia won't act immediately. He savors his revenge. We know that. We've studied him for years."

Elena wouldn't let herself think about the ways a cruel man would *savor* revenge. Instead she looked at the ceiling, thinking of the important government people searching for her upstairs, determined to find her. She wasn't afraid of them or Kriloff anymore. She was only afraid that Audubon would die.

The fax machine hummed again. Elena and Clarice hunched over it. Elena's eyes burned from staring at the paper creeping out. "Ah, Traynor," Clarice said with a thoughtful tone, as *Bird Dog* appeared in fluid, scrolled script. "He's in charge. He's our top person."

*Status on Dove requested*, the message read. *I say use her. Why the change in plans?*

Elena staggered a little and stepped back. Clarice followed quickly and grabbed her arms. "Let me explain."

"I'm the dove. I was supposed to be used as . . . as what?"

"A trade. A bargaining chip. Audubon could have turned you over to the State Department in exchange for help in getting Kash out of Mexico."

Elena shut her eyes, feeling numb. She'd known all along there was a hidden motive to his kindness, but it hurt to hear it confirmed. She looked at Clarice again. "But he didn't turn me over."

"No. He went to Mexico and traded *himself*. I'll tell you something else. He left arrangements for you to have all the money you'll need to settle in America and make a good life." Clarice was crying now. "He loves you so much. Please understand he would never have hurt you. Even if he'd gone through with his plan, he'd have made certain you weren't sent back to Russia. He loves you so much that he's giving up his life!"

"Will you bring me a glass of water, please? I feel faint."

"Sit down, honey. I'll be right back."

As soon as Clarice disappeared down a hallway to a small kitchen, Elena turned and ran for the stairs. At the top she pushed a button, and the panel slid back. Calmly, smoothing her hands over her hair and dress, she walked out of Audubon's study into the main hall. A startled FBI agent dropped his walkie-talkie.

"I am Elena Petrovic," she told him.

In less than two minutes a dozen men surrounded her. *I must be very valuable, indeed. Good.* The agent in charge gave her the coolest of scrutiny. "For a secretary, you've certainly caused the State Department a lot of money, time, and embarrassment."

"I'll end all the trouble and go back to Kriloff." She glanced over the man's shoulder. In the background Clarice and Bernard watched with shattered expressions. "On one condition: Your government must bring T. S. Audubon back from Mexico alive."

"You don't have much to bargain with, Ms. Petrovic."

"Oh? Several important people know my story—the poor young woman, trying to defect, only to find that your government is more interested in making a famous Russian scientist happy by returning his secretary to him, even though she begs for freedom."

The agent scowled, but she could tell he was willing to negotiate. She smiled sadly at Clarice. *I also will give up my life.*


To Audubon's dazed vision the stars seemed to have been smeared across the night sky. His focus was coming back slowly. He knew that he was in pain, that the ground where he lay was sandy but not soft enough for his bruised body, that a small cactus was sticking him in the arm. The sticking sensation ended. Amused but gentle voices were discussing him.

"Let the pain medication get into his bloodstream, and five minutes from now he'll be giving us a lecture on tactical negotiations."

"Or asking for a bottle of cognac and a violin."

"He won't be playing the violin for a while."

"You know my father better than that. He'll be playing Mozart by tomorrow."

Audubon opened his eyes and met Kash's gaze. With his darkly exotic looks the young man belonged in a desert, but not this one. He should be dressed like a sheikh, Audubon thought groggily, not wearing a dusty khaki shirt and trousers. A sheikh for a son. He loved the idea. He loved Kash.

"Father," Kash said gently, pressing a hand into his shoulder, "it's all over. Everything is all right."

"Dead?" They both knew who he meant.

"No, he got away from us. We were lucky to surprise his people when we did. If we hadn't had help . . . well, never mind."

"Help?"

"The cavalry arrived just in time," the other voice said. Jeopard Surprise was kneeling beside him, also, he realized.

Audubon licked his sunburned lips. "Cavalry?"

Kash patted his shoulder. "We'll explain after you've been patched up, Father."

"Father. You never called me that before."

"Well, you never tried so hard to get yourself killed before. I'd better say all the things I've wanted to say for years, because you seem to be getting reckless . . . I love you."

"I love you too."

"Traynor says you didn't have to risk your life for me."

"Traynor is a cynic."

"I heard that," Traynor said from somewhere. "My feelings are hurt."

"You have no feelings. That's why I hired you."

"Birds of a feather, Chief, birds of a feather."

"Not me. Not anymore." Audubon drew his first deep breath without pain stabbing his ribs. *Elena.* From the moment he'd regained consciousness, she'd been dancing at the edges of his mind, a promise that had been fulfilled beyond his best hopes. Not only had he saved his son, he was alive and going home to Elena.

"How soon can we get out of here?" he asked Kash. "I have someone important for you to meet back at home."

There was silence for a moment, filled with the night wind whipping along empty earth. Audubon's vision was clear now. He looked from Jeopard to Kash, not liking the troubled glances they exchanged.

"Let me tell him," Jeopard said finally. "It should come from someone who knew her."

Paris. All she saw of it from the plane's small window was other planes taxiing across gray concrete. The sky was the same color of gray. Nearly the same shade as her awful gray suit. Much lighter than her mood.

She pressed her forehead against the warm glass and let misery overwhelm her again, until she was quivering. At least they'd transferred from an American military plan to a commercial flight. But Kriloff and his group were the flight's only occupants and there would be no return for her. Sergei patted her hand. "When we get back to the institute, I'll make you some fish head soup, Laney-kitten. You'll feel better then."

"No. But my friend was rescued. That's all that matters." When she thought about never seeing Audubon again, never hearing his voice or making love to him or having the chance to learn all the mysteries she'd wanted to know, she didn't care what happened next.

"She'll come to her senses," Kriloff said. He lounged at the front of the first-class cabin, surveying the KGB bodyguards scattered around him in the plush seats. Finally his eyes met Elena's deadly stare. "What kind of future did T. S. Audubon offer you? Marriage? No. He would have exploited you and your gift then tossed you out when he grew bored."

"He gave me more love and respect than you can ever understand. He is a man of tradition and honor."

"Tradition and honor?" The doctor laughed. "Do you want to hear what he did to his parents when he was eighteen years old?"

She stiffened. "How would you know?"

"I had much time to learn about the man, Elena."

"Oh, who really knows the truth about such old tales?" Sergei interjected, sounding regretful and patting her hand anxiously. "We don't need to talk about—"

"You're in enough trouble, Sergei, without adding insubordination to it." Kriloff glared at him, not used to having a bodyguard voice an opinion to his face. Elena clutched Sergei's hand. He would probably be demoted for letting her get away that night at the hotel in Richmond. The night she'd met Audubon. Her throat burned with tears. "What are you trying to tell me about Audubon?" she asked Kriloff coolly. "I know everything that's important."

"Elena, you are so naive. The man murdered his own mother and father."

She sat back slowly, as if a giant invisible hand were flattening her against the seat. For a second, she couldn't breathe. Sergei leaned close and whispered, "Accused but found innocent."

"Sergei, *be quiet*," Kriloff said. He went to the seat across from them and sat down casually, crossing his legs. "Audubon was responsible for his own sister's death too. Imagine. A twelve-year-old boy deliberately pushing his younger sister off of a ski lift."

Sergei squeezed her hand. *More lies,* he was telling her. Elena shoved her fists into the pockets of her baggy gray jacket. "I'd like to have heard the *true* story from Audubon. Not your version." Her fingers closed around the funny wooden turtle she'd managed to keep. The smooth surface had been polished by Audubon's fingers for years. A sense of certainty and peace flowed from it.

What a tragic story he would have told her, if she'd been able to stay with him. She would have been a sympathetic listener. She hoped, wherever he was right now, that he could feel her loving him.

All conversation stopped as a tall, slender young man wearing a flight attendant's uniform stepped inside the cabin. "Good afternoon," he said in French. His teeth flashed white against an olive complexion. His features were handsome and unusual, a puzzling mixture of nationalities. His hair was glossy black. But when he smiled at Elena, she wasn't sure if she smiled back. She was already lost in thoughts about Audubon again.

"The crew will be boarding soon," the handsome attendant continued. "But in the meantime I'd like to tell you about our in-flight movie." He reached inside his jacket, produced a pistol, and pointed it at Kriloff. "It's called *Return of the Dove*. Ms. Petrovic, I'll be happy to escort you out."

She stared at him. Kash Santelli. Of course! But where was Audubon? *They lied to you. He's dead.* Kash had dutifully come here to fulfill his dead father's wishes.

"I'll simply follow you back to America and retrieve her again," Kriloff said.

Elena stood. She spoke slowly and calmly, because

she was hollow inside. "No, you won't. I have nothing left to lose. I'll tell everything. I'll create the most terrible scandal you can imagine. I'll let the whole world know that you keep people locked up and study them like laboratory animals. And I'll be sure to tell them that you make your prize subjects produce children together, to see if miracles are genetic." She nodded at the anger in Kash Santelli's dark eyes. "If I go back to the institute, I'm scheduled to be artificially inseminated, like a cow."

"Are you ready to leave?" a man behind Kash asked, stepping into the cabin. Elena didn't recognize him. He was brawny and auburn-haired, and he held a gun against the front of his baggage handler's jumpsuit. He didn't look as if he needed the gun to terrify people. "I'll keep this nice little group seated."

Elena eased past Sergei, stroking his mottled cheek as she did. He kissed her hand. "I'm going to defect! I'll get off the plane here, after you leave."

"Come to America and meet me," she told him. "We'll be family."

"Yes!"

She looked at Kriloff. He was grinding his teeth and shivering with fury. "Follow me, and I'll ruin you," she whispered.

A few seconds later she was walking swiftly across the tarmac with Kash Santelli, not speaking, afraid freedom was an illusion that would end before it began. Like her life with Audubon. She hugged herself as Kash guided her into a small car. "We have a flight to catch," he said cheerfully, driving like a madman between planes and baggage carts.

She looked wearily out the window, unconcerned. "Is Audubon dead?"

"Dead? Of course not! Why did you think so?"

She jerked to attention. "But why didn't he—oh, I'm so greedy. Of course, he didn't have to meet me here, himself."

"Put your head on your knees. I don't want anyone to see you."

She clutched her knees for several minutes, swaying

with the car, humming under her breath. He was alive! If he hadn't made a dramatic rescue in person, what did it matter? Her blood froze. This was not like Audubon at all. "He's hurt," she said numbly.

Kash slid the car to a squealing halt. She glanced at the small jet next to them, then turned toward him. "Tell me."

"Yes, but he'll be fine, now that he's got you back."

She was full of questions and fear as she climbed the jet's stairway. Kyle Surprise grasped her hand and pulled her in. "Welcome to Audubon Airlines. We'll be on our way to Scotland in about sixty seconds."

"Traynor's holding the fort," Kash said. "He'll meet us later."

She looked around fervently, seeing nothing but the cockpit door, Kyle, Drake Lancaster, and thick curtains that closed off the jet's cabin. She reached for them wildly.

"Be careful when you hug him," Kash urged, pulling the curtains back. "He'll need at least a month before he's huggable—wait!"

But she was already running toward Audubon, who was propped up in a thronelike pair of cushioned seats, smiling at her and holding out a hand as best he could. His face was covered in bruises, and the thick binding around his rib cage showed through his white shirt.

She shrieked something, his name or a blessing, or both, she didn't know, but she was making hoarse little sounds in her throat as she climbed into a corner of one seat and pressed as much of her body against him as she could.

"No, love, don't," he begged hoarsely, as she ran her hands over his chest, pouring her warmth and energy into him.

"Elena, you're hurting him," Kash said firmly. He took her shoulders. "Come sit down . . ." His voice trailed off. "It feels as if I just put my hands into a warm bath. My God."

She murmured Audubon's name and put her hands

on his face. Audubon kissed her hands but kept repeating desperately. "I'm all right. Don't make yourself sick. I love you. I don't want to hurt you."

"I know," she whispered, feeling his body mending, bound to him with an energy that she knew, for the first time, she could control because of him. "I'm fine. I'm free, and I'm with you. You'll be able to hold me while I sleep."

"Elena." He put his arms around her, moving with a limberness he hadn't been capable of only seconds before. "I'll hold you forever."


She knew she was in trouble before she opened her eyes. She was in another sinfully plush bed, in a room scented with flowers. And Audubon was sitting beside her, tracing her mouth with his fingertip.

She blinked lazily and looked up at him. "You're perfect again," she whispered. "Inside and out."

The smile he gave her had its own sensual power. She glanced lower and saw that he wore a heavy, blue satin dressing gown. A handsome portion of his chest showed between the lapels. The leg that was drawn up beside her was deliciously bare.

"I hope that we're someplace decadent," she said.

"Not decadent, but definitely Victorian. We're at Elgiva and Douglas's estate on the Scottish coast."

"I missed everything."

"Yes, you put on quite a show, draped in my arms like Sleeping Beauty. All the servants are probably gossiping about the way I carried you straight up here. And Kash kept staring at his hands, then at the two of us, particularly me. On the plane, when I took off my rib bandages, I thought he was going to need help with his jaw. It seemed to be permanently hinged open."

She touched the voluminous flannel gown she wore. It was buttoned up to her neck. "Elgiva's?"

"Yes. She said she knows it's not appealing, but that old Scottish manors are *drrrafty*. Hmmm." He ran his fingers down the buttons at the center of her chest. "Actually, the interesting texture and deceptively proper appearance are *very* appealing."

Elena took his hand and held it against her cheek, loving the feel of the weathered skin. The tenderness inside her was reflected in his own eyes. They sat quietly, smiling at each other. "You saved my life, Elena."

"You saved mine."

"Clarice said you didn't hesitate, even after you learned the truth."

"About you intending to trade me to the State Department to get help for your son? That's not such an awful truth to learn, Audubon."

"Even if I'd gone through with it, I would have made certain you weren't sent back to Russia."

"I know." She stroked the back of his hand, making her touch intentionally soothing. "I know the truth about your family also. I don't have a very clear picture of what happened, but enough to understand how terrible it must have been for you."

He gave her a troubled look. "Who told you?"

"Kriloff. He investigated your background."

"What did he say?"

"That you were a murderer."

"You didn't wonder if—"

"No, I didn't. Sergei said you were found innocent, but even if he hadn't told me that, I wouldn't have thought you capable of harming your own parents."

Audubon took her hands and held them against his chest. She felt the steady, slow beat of his heart. It was a wonderful heart, incapable of anything ugly. She knew that without having to touch him. "I trust you," she reminded him.

He exhaled slowly. "My family went skiing in Switzerland every winter. By the time I was twelve and my sister was ten, we were experts. We were also Audubons, which meant that we were arrogant, hardheaded, and spoiled. Our parents always went their own way and left us under the watch of some poor, abused nanny. On this occasion we sneaked away from her and went to the slopes by ourselves."

"We should never have been allowed to ride up on the lift without an adult, but we were the rich, over-confident Audubons, and none of the ski lodge employees wanted to risk making our parents angry. So they let us go."

He shut his eyes. Elena saw the pain around them. "We were pushing at each other, just playing, nothing foolish, I swear. One second Melinda was beside me, and the next . . . she was falling."

"Oh, Audubon."

"I could never decide if I caused her to fall or if it was just a freak accident. For years I played it over and over in my mind. It nearly drove me crazy."

"It was an accident."

He looked at her curiously. "I found one of my paperweights in the pocket of your suit. Why did you pick up that particular piece?"

"I wanted something of yours that was personal. I took it on my way downstairs to hide, when the government men came. I'd just learned that you might be killed in Mexico. The wooden turtle looked warm and friendly to me. And quiet, as if it had been around for years and had nothing to prove."

"My sister carved it. She was so creative. I'm sure she would have been an artist or sculptor if she'd lived."

"I think she loved you very much, and you loved her, and that what happened wasn't from carelessness on your part. It could have been you who fell, just as easily."

"I learned to believe that, eventually." He looked at her sadly. "My parents never did, though."

"They blamed you?"

"Yes. I was the older child, and the boy. That made me responsible for what happened. My mother, who claimed to be psychic, said that she'd dreamed that I hated Melinda. That was the opposite of the truth. Melinda and I were so obnoxious in all the same ways that we adored each other. But Mother trusted her dream more than she trusted me. I was banished, you might say, to one of the strictest military academies in Virginia. From the time I was twelve years old, I came home only for holidays and a few weeks during the summer. I can't say that there wasn't some relief in being away from them. I think they'd disliked each other for years before the accident. Afterward, the relationship only got worse."

"And when you were eighteen . . ." Her throat closed. She stared at him, waiting.

"I was home temporarily, getting ready to leave for college. It was the first time I realized how violent my parents had become toward each other. Throwing things, screaming at each other. One night I came home from a party and . . . found them. There was a gun." She saw a muscle flex convulsively in his throat. "Both of them. Dead."

Elena sat up and put her arms around him. "How could anyone accuse you?"

"There was never any serious case against me, not even an indictment, just lurid newspaper articles and a lot of gossip about the bitterness in the family. The coroner's report made it clear that no third party was involved in what happened."

Audubon hugged her hard and said with strained lightness, "So that's the sordid story of my family. Honestly, it won't hurt my feelings if you double-check the details."

"I've already seen the proof. I declare you innocent. Case closed." She sat back, wiping her eyes. "And now I understand why you don't think much of the idea of marrying and having a family."

The old memories faded from his eyes. His expression gentled so much that she became very still, almost enchanted. "I was afraid *you* wouldn't think much of marriage—at least not in connection with me—after hearing my story."

Under the solemn flannel, her heart began to race. "I remember a discussion once about bookstores, dogs, and cats. Marriage was mentioned briefly, but it never stood a chance."

"Bookstores, dogs, cats, marriage, children. It all goes together in my mind."

"But you have a very manipulative mind, dear man."

"But I thought you'd learned to enjoy that about me, dear woman."

"Is this a marriage proposal?"

"I've never been involved in one before, but, yes, I believe that's what it is." Growing serious, he took her face between his hands. "Elena, please marry me."

"Please kiss me." He did. "Yes."

"Please say yes again, and dress it up."

"I love you with every bit of my heart, and I'll make flowers bloom for you as long as I live."

"Nice," he whispered, pulling her into his arms. "Very nice dressing up."

Much later, in the quiet, she reminded him that he'd promised to tell her his full name. He smiled against her lips. "I promise to tell you on your eightieth birthday, when all of our children and grandchildren are gathered around to hear. It should be a dramatic moment."

She laughed softly. This fox would always be sly. Still, she wouldn't mind the wait.

# THE EDITOR'S CORNER

Each month we have LOVESWEPTs that dazzle . . . that warm the heart or bring laughter and the occasional tear—all of them sensual and full of love, of course. Seldom, however, are all six books literally sizzling with so much fiery passion and tumultuous romance as next month's.

First, a love story sure to blaze in your memory is remarkable Billie Green's **STARBRIGHT,** LOVESWEPT #456. Imagine a powerful man with midnight-blue eyes and a former model who has as much heart and soul as she does beauty. He is brilliant lawyer Garrick Fane, a man with a secret. She is Elise Adler Bright, vulnerable and feisty, who believes Garrick has betrayed her. When a terrifying accident hurls them together, they have one last chance to explore their fierce physical love . . . and the desperate problems each has tried to hide. As time runs out for them, they must recapture the true love they'd once believed was theirs—or lose it forever. Fireworks sparked with humor. A sizzler, indeed.

Prepare to soar when you read LOVESWEPT #457, **PASSION'S FLIGHT,** by talented Terry Lawrence. Sensual, sensual, sensual is this story of a legendary dancer and notorious seducer known throughout the world as "Stash." He finds the woman he can love faithfully for a lifetime in Mariah Heath. Mariah is also a dancer and one Stash admires tremendously for her grace and fierce emotionality. But he is haunted by a past that closes him to enduring love—and Mariah must struggle to break through her own vulnerabilities to teach her incredible lover that forever can be theirs. This is a romance that's as unforgettable as it is delectable.

As steamy as the bayou, as exciting as Bourbon Street in New Orleans, **THE RESTLESS HEART,** LOVESWEPT #458, by gifted Tami Hoag, is sure to win your heart. Tami has really given us a gift in the hero she's created for this romance. What a wickedly handsome, mischievous, and sexy Cajun Remy Doucet is! And how he woos heroine Danielle Hamilton. From diapering babies to kissing a lady senseless, Remy is masterful. But a lie and a shadow stand between him and Danielle . . . and only when a dangerous misunderstanding parts them can they find truth and the love they deserve. Reading not to be missed!

Guaranteed to start a real conflagration in your imagination is extraordinary Sandra Chastain's **FIREBRAND,** LOVESWEPT #459. Cade McCall wasn't the kind of man to answer an ad as mysterious as Rusty Wilder's—but he'd never needed a job so badly. When he met the green-eyed rancher whose wild red hair echoed her spirit, he fell hard. Rusty found Cade too handsome, too irresistible to become the partner she needed. Consumed by the flames of desire they generated, only searing romance could follow . . . but each feared their love might turn to ashes if he or she couldn't tame the other. Silk and denim . . . fire and ice. A LOVESWEPT that couldn't have been better titled—**FIREBRAND.**

Delightful Janet Evanovich outdoes herself with **THE ROCKY ROAD TO ROMANCE,** LOVESWEPT #460, which sparkles with fiery fun. In the midst of a wild and woolly romantic chase between Steve Crow and Daisy Adams, you should be prepared to meet an old and fascinating friend—that quirky Elsie Hawkins. This is Elsie's fourth appearance in Janet's LOVESWEPTS. All of us have come to look forward to where she'll turn up next . . . and just how she'll affect the outcome of a stalled romance. Elsie won't disappoint you as she works her wondrous ways on the smoldering romance of Steve and Daisy. A real winner!

Absolutely breathtaking! A daring love story not to be missed! Those were just a couple of the remarks heard in the office from those who read **TABOO**, LOVESWEPT #461, by Olivia Rupprecht. Cammie Walker had been adopted by Grant Kennedy's family when her family died in a car crash. She grew up with great brotherly love for Grant. Then, one night when Cammie came home to visit, she saw Grant as she'd never seen him before. Her desire for him was overwhelming . . . unbearably so. And Grant soon confessed he'd been passionately in love with her for years. But Cammie was terrified of their love . . . and terrified of how it might affect her adopted parents. **TABOO** is one of the most emotionally touching and stunningly sensual romances of the year.

And do make sure you look for the three books next month in Bantam's fabulous imprint, FANFARE . . . the very best in women's popular fiction. It's a spectacular FANFARE month with **SCANDAL** by Amanda Quick, **STAR-CROSSED LOVERS** by Kay Hooper, and **HEAVEN SENT** by newcomer Pamela Morsi.

Enjoy!

Sincerely,

*Carolyn Nichols*

Carolyn Nichols,
Publisher,
*LOVESWEPT*
Bantam Books
666 Fifth Avenue
New York, NY 10103

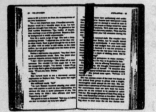